Shakti

Shakti
51 Sacred Peethas of the Goddess

ALKA PANDE

Published by
Rupa Publications India Pvt. Ltd 2020
7/16, Ansari Road, Daryaganj
New Delhi 110002

Sales centres:
Bengaluru Chennai
Hyderabad Jaipur Kathmandu
Kolkata Mumbai Prayagraj

Copyright © Alka Pande 2020

The views and opinions expressed in this book are the authors' own and the facts are as reported by her which have been verified to the extent possible, and the publishers are not in any way liable for the same.

All rights reserved.
No part of this publication may be reproduced, transmitted, or stored in a retrieval system, in any form or by any means, electronic, mechanical, photocopying, recording or otherwise, without the prior permission of the publisher.

P-ISBN: 978-93-90356-49-2
E-ISBN: 978-93-90356-57-7

Third impression 2025

10 9 8 7 6 5 4 3

The moral right of the author has been asserted.

Printed in India

This book is sold subject to the condition that it shall not, by way of trade or otherwise, be lent, resold, hired out, or otherwise circulated, without the publisher's prior consent, in any form of binding or cover other than that in which it is published.

*To my mother, Kamala Pande,
the most powerful Shakti*

Contents

Mapping the Sacred Dwellings of Shakti — xi

1. Bhabanipur Shakti Peetha — 1
   Karatoya, Bhabanipur, Bangladesh

2. Avanti Shakti Peetha — 5
   Bhairava Parvat, Ujjain, Madhya Pradesh

3. Bahula Shakti Peetha — 9
   Ketugram, Katwa, West Bengal

4. Triambakeshwar Bhramari Devi Shakti Peetha — 13
   Panchvati, Nasik, Maharashtra

5. Brajeshwari Devi Shakti Peetha — 17
   Kangra, Himachal Pradesh

6. Chhinnamastika Devi Shakti Peetha — 22
   Chintpurni, Una District, Himachal Pradesh

7. Dakshayani Devi Shakti Peetha — 27
   Manas, Tibet

8. Gandaki Devi Shakti Peetha — 30
   Muktinath, Nepal

9. Jashoreshwari Devi Shakti Peetha — 35
   Jessore, Bangladesh

10. Jayanti Devi Shakti Peetha — 40
    Jaintia Hills, Meghalaya

11. Jwalaji Shakti Peetha *Kangra, Himachal Pradesh*	44
12. Kalmadhav Devi Shakti Peetha *Amarkantak, Madhya Pradesh*	48
13. Kamakhya Devi Shakti Peetha *Kamgiri, Assam*	52
14. Kankalitala Devi Shakti Peetha *Bolpur, West Bengal*	58
15. Kanyashram Shakti Peetha *Kanyakumari, Tamil Nadu*	62
16. Kiriteshwari Devi Shakti Peetha *Murshidabad, West Bengal*	67
17. Kottari Devi Shakti Peetha *Hinglaj, Pakistan*	71
18. Mahamaya Shakti Peetha *Amarnath, Jammu and Kashmir*	77
19. Phullara Devi Shakti Peetha *Attahas, West Bengal*	83
20. Ratnavali Shakti Peetha *Hooghly, West Bengal*	87
21. Mahishamardini Shakti Peetha *Birbhum, West Bengal*	90
22. Chamundeshwari Shakti Peetha *Mysuru, Karnataka*	94
23. Katyayani Shakti Peetha *Vrindavan, Uttar Pradesh*	99
24. Vishalakshi Shakti Peetha *Varanasi, Uttar Pradesh*	103

25. Kalighat Shakti Peetha — 107
    Kolkata, West Bengal

26. Jogadya Shakti Peetha — 112
    Kshirgram, West Bengal

27. Umakotilingeshwara Swamy or
    Godavari Tir Shakti Peetha — 115
    Rajahmundry, Andhra Pradesh

28. Panchasagar Shakti Peetha — 120
    Varanasi, Uttar Pradesh

29. Devi Danteshwari Shakti Peetha — 123
    Bastar, Chhattisgarh

30. Srisailam Shakti Peetha — 127
    Srisailam, Andhra Pradesh

31. Nandikeshwari Shakti Peetha — 132
    Birbhum, West Bengal

32. Uma Shakti Peetha — 135
    Mithila, Bihar

33. Tara Tarini Shakti Peetha — 138
    Ganjam, Odisha

34. Mangala Gauri Shakti Peetha — 143
    Gaya, Bihar

35. Shivani Devi Shakti Peetha — 146
    Ramagiri, Uttar Pradesh

36. Sharada Devi Shakti Peetha — 149
    Maihar, Madhya Pradesh

37. Mangal Chandika Shakti Peetha — 154
    Ujjain, Madhya Pradesh

38. Lalita Devi Shakti Peetha — 158
    Prayagraj, Uttar Pradesh

39. Devagarbha Shakti Peetha — 161
   Kanchipuram, Tamil Nadu

40. Guhyeshwari Shakti Peetha — 165
   Kathmandu, Nepal

41. Narmada Shakti Peetha — 169
   Amarkantak, Madhya Pradesh

42. Bargabhima Devi Shakti Peetha — 174
   East Midnapore, West Bengal

43. Bhadrakali Shakti Peetha — 178
   Kurukshetra, Haryana

44. Tripura Sundari Shakti Peetha — 182
   Udaipur, Tripura

45. Kalika Shakti Peetha — 187
   Pavagadh, Gujarat

46. Vimala Devi Shakti Peetha — 191
   Puri, Odisha

47. Sugandha Devi Shakti Peetha — 195
   Shikarpur, Bangladesh

48. Tripurmalini Devi Shakti Peetha — 198
   Jalandhar, Punjab

49. Indrakshi Shakti Peetha — 201
   Manipallavam, Sri Lanka

50. Shivaharkaray Shakti Peetha — 205
   Karavipur, Karachi, Pakistan

51. Chandrabhaga Shakti Peetha — 208
   Prabhas, Girna Hills, Gujarat

Acknowledgements — 211
Bibliography — 213

Mapping the Sacred Dwellings of Shakti

Obeisance be to Her who is pure Being-Consciousness-Bliss. As Power, who exists in the form of Time and Space and all that is therein, who is the radiant Illuminatrix in all beings.

—YOGINI HRIDAYA TANTRA

India's cultural tradition is immersed deeply in myths and stories, where the Puranic tales have become part of the religious and cultural tradition of the country. Mythology is the main component of religion, which consists of stories and folklores on various gods and goddesses. Within the Indian tradition, there are a number of stories or myths associated with a single god or goddess. In the case of mapping or tracing the 51 sacred spaces where Shakti dwells, the origins of the abodes are shrouded in a number of tales, which can be interpreted by the bhakta in the way he/she wishes to trace the evolution. This is truly the beauty of Sanatan dharma—the very backbone of inclusive Hindu thought.

When we think of Shakti, the first thought and image that comes to mind is the all-powerful Durga astride her tiger. She is seated comfortably on the dangerous beast, signalling to everyone that the might of the tiger is completely under her control. Yet another potent image is that of Kali, her tongue coated with fresh blood, naked, her hair unbound, standing on top of an inert, primordial Shiva, wearing a garland of skulls that fall on her voluptuous breasts. *Devi Sahastranam* is a living text of the number of avataras or forms Shakti has been transformed into, which are more then 1,001.

Sifting through the many layers of myths, I would like to be clear about the trajectory I am creating in my journey to the affirmation of the feminine power of Shakti, where she emerged from, and how Sati becomes one of her manifestations in a saguna, or form, and how as Sati, she spreads her area of power and strength in her 51 dwellings. In order to do this, I have to go back to her very origins:

> *Ya devi sarvabhuteshu buddhi rupena samsthitaa*
> *Namastasyai namastasyai namastasyai namo namaha*

[To that goddess who dwells within all beings in the form of intellect, I bow again and again and again.]

—CHANDI PATH (DEVI MAHATMYA), CH. 5, V. 20

I am in fact closing on to one aspect of Shakti, which is the story/myth of Sati, one of the 24 daughters of Daksha and his wife Prasuti, the daughter of Manu and Shatarupa. In another story, it is said that Daksha had another wife called Panchajani or Virini, and that Sati was their child. All 24 daughters were different aspects of Shakti. Sati was supposedly the youngest and was also the manifestation of Truth. All his daughters had special attributes:

1. Sraddha (Respect)
2. Bhakti (Worship)
3. Dhriti (Steadiness)
4. Thushti (Resignation)
5. Pushti (Thriving)
6. Medha (Intelligence)
7. Kriya (Action, Devotion)
8. Buddhika (Intellect)

9. Lajja Gauri (Modesty)
10. Vapu (Body)
11. Santi (Expiation)
12. Siddhika (Perfection)
13. Kirtti (Fame)
14. Khyati (Celebrity)
15. Sati (Truth)
16. Sambhuti (Fitness)
17. Smriti (Memory)
18. Priti (Affection)
19. Kshama (Forgiveness)
20. Sannati (Humility)
21. Anasuya (Without jealousy)
22. Urjja (Energy)
23. Swaha (Offering)
24. Swadha (Oblation)

Who, then, was Daksha—the man who sired these 24 Shaktis? Daksha himself was one of the four sons of Brahma and Aditi. We know of Brahma as part of the Holy Indian Trinity, which consists of Brahma, Vishnu and Shiva. Brahma is known as the creator, Vishnu the preserver and Shiva the destroyer. There are again myths as to the origin of Brahma himself. One Puranic myth states that he was also svayambhu or self-born, the creative aspect of Vishnu; he was Vagisa, the lord of speech; and as Vedanatha, he was creator of the four Vedas, one from each of his four mouths, hence also Chaturmukha. Brahma is also synonymous with the Vedic god, Prajapati, and his consort is Saraswati.

The Mother Earth created his ten mind-born sons or mana putras, after which the four kumaras—Daksha, Dharma, Kamadeva and Agni—were created from his body parts: the right thumb, chest, heart and eyebrows, respectively. Even the visual iconography highlights him as an obese man with a stocky body, protruding belly, and the head of an ibex-like creature with spiral horns. In yet another interpretation, Daksha is one of the 11 prajapatis, the abled one and also the skilled one.

Sati, who was also known as Dakshayani, was his youngest daughter and, much against her father's wishes, married Shiva, who was intensely disliked by Daksha. He thought that Shiva was a dirty, ugly ascetic with an army of ghouls, dopers and unkempt ruffians. The story of *Daksha Yagna Nasha* finds mention in a number of Puranas like *Vayu Purana, Skanda Purana, Kurma Purna, Harivamsa Purana, Padma Purana, Longa Purana, Shiva Purana* and *Matsaya Purana*.

THE LEGEND OF SATI

Soon after her marriage to Shiva, Daksha organized a massive yagna to which he invited all his sons-in-law, the devas and powerful sages. According to *Bhagavat Purana*, Marichi and the other saptrishis (the seven sages), along with Daksha, had organized a significant yagna that had all the powerful devas present. Marichi was himself one of the mind-born sons of Brahma and one of the saptrishis from whom all the Brahmins of India descend. It is also accepted that he is the founder of Vedanta and in one of his incarnations was also Mahavira, the twenty-fourth Tirthankar. As the celestial patriarch, Daksha was also the head of the sacrifice, and resplendent and shining like the sun, impressed and overawed the august assembly. Everyone got up to greet the great and powerful Daksha but not Shiva. Seeing this, Daksha was enraged as his huge ego was trampled upon by Shiva not rising in his presence. He cursed Shiva and left for his home. Shiva remained unaffected. The seeds of conflict between Shiva and Daksha were sown by this act. Over a period of time, Brahma declared Daksha to be the first amongst the patriarchs. This further added to the ego of Daksha, making him even more arrogant and haughty. Soon after his elevation, Daksha performed the Vaajapeya sacrifice and then decided to perform the biggest sacrifice of all—the Bhrihaspati Sava sacrifice—with all the glory and pomp it required. Hectic preparations and a massive number of invitations were all being organized. Sati came to know of this colossal ceremony and got very excited and made up her mind to be part of this event.

As the preparations increased and Sati witnessed the many celestial participants to the yagna, she was surprised that there was no invitation for her and her husband Shiva. Not that this had any effect on Shiva, but when Sati insisted on going, Shiva was not at all pleased. Sati however, asserted her wish and went uninvited to the yagna. On reaching the big ceremony, Sati realized how her own father had deliberately humiliated her and her beloved husband Shiva. She felt demeaned and in absolute mortification, jumped into the sacrificial fire.

When Shiva heard of Sati's self-immolation, he was beside himself with sorrow and rage. The infuriated Shiva took the form of Veerbhadra, meaning 'born out of the hair of Shiva'. Placing Sati's body across his shoulder, he embarked on the dance of death formally known as Tandava. So worried were the gods that Narayana himself intervened. Using his powerful weapon, the Sudarshana Chakra, he cut the body of Sati into numerous parts. Some say there were 108 parts; however, I am limiting myself to the 51 parts that are the more acceptable figure. Over a period of time, they came to be known as the 51 Peethas, or sacred spots, where Sati's body parts fell. Once Sati's body was dismembered, Shiva finally became quiet and went back to Mount Kailasha. This story lays the ground for the emergence of the Shakti Peethas.

While exploring the story of the Shakti Peethas I found myself drawn to the concept of the body i.e. sharira, the concept of Peetha or teerthas, the rituals of worship culminating in the prasada or the offering of the bhakta and then the consumption of the prasada by the bhaktas themselves. The Shakti cult was a later addition to the Hindu Trinity, because for Daksha's yagna, all the Vedic deities were invited except Shiva, who soon acquired authority as the Vedic Rudra's successor.

BODY/SHARIRA

The body is a rather special and nuanced concept in the Indian philosophical context. There are multiple meanings and layers in which it is enshrined. The sharira is the vessel or the form that is the receptacle of the atman. It becomes an instrument of the atman. Thus, it is also transient and ephemeral. The body is also made up of the panchbhootas/panchtattavas—the five elements—and is also associated with impurity. At a physical level, it has a form and a structure. The quest for the cosmic world begins from the panchtattavas: prithvi (earth), jal (water), agni (fire), vayu (air) and akasha (ether). In Indian mythology, the universe, in harmony with the five elements, is the ideal state of working. Collectively, these form the life force, which later disintegrates to the celestial cores. These panchtattavas are aligned to our sensorial sensitivities—ears, skin, eyes, tongue and nose—which aid the process of the five physical perceptions of this universe: sound, touch, sight, taste and smell.

As the abode of the atman, the body serves as an expansion of the Supreme Soul. As stated earlier, the body consists of each of the panchatattvas. *Amar Kosha, Garbhaopanishad and Maitri Upanishad* are a few of the pre-modern books of Indic wisdom which explain and explore the many meanings of sharira, which is also known as deha. The body also becomes the form through which the adoration of the divine as 'saguna' becomes explicit and therefore extremely important in Hinduism. It is through saguna that the rituals and religion in India are expressed. God is in the image of man.

Post the Puranic period, the abstract philosophical notion of God underwent a complete transformation including the

Shakti cult. The iconographies started taking shape around her form and Sati as Shakti found her own representation. Their image-makers started creating their own interpretations of Shiva carrying the corpse of Sati.

SHAKTI PEETHA/TEERTHA

Originating from Sanskrit, the word 'Peetha' means 'seat, altar, shrine or dwelling'. In the case of the Shakti Peethas, it is very specific. It is the sacred space where the Supreme Goddess takes a strong, well-founded seat on Earth. Each of the Peethas have been turned into shrines for the Goddess by the very people who believe in the absolute power of the feminine. Each site where the 51 body parts of Sati fell, came to be known as a Shakti Peetha.

A teertha is a crossing. As with most Sanskrit words, there are multiple meanings of this too. Teertha is also the passing of the atman to the parmatman the crossing from the physical world to the metaphysical world. These 51 sacred sites are also linked by theologists and scholars to the 51 alphabets of the Sanskrit language. In each of the Peethas also resides Kaalbhairava, which is another name of Shiva. Most of the Shakti Peetha shrines contain a naturally appearing stone which becomes the object of worship around which the temple shrine is built.

Vindhyavasini is an additional Shakti Peetha, which I have deliberately not included in the 51 Peethas. While a powerful dwelling of Shakti, Vindhyavasini is not the abode of Shakti as Sati's body parts. It is, however, the preferred choice and home of Yogamaya, the sister of Krishna, who escaped from Kamsa's prison at Mathura.

Kalika Purana indicates that there are four Adi Shakti Peethas, which is further affirmed in the commentary and text of *Brihat Samhita*. It lists the names of the location at various places in India such as Vimla temple, Odisha, where her feet fell, Tara Tarini temple in Behrampur, Odisha, where her breasts fell, Kamakhya temple in Guwahati, Assam, where her yoni or vagina fell and lastly, the Kalighat temple in West Bengal, where her right toe fell.

THE ICONOGRAPHY OF THE DEVI

Since antiquity, Goddess worship has been part of the Indic tradition of India. In fact, the Goddess is even more popular than Shiva and Vishnu. All the manifestations, avataras or appearances of the many forms of Devi belong to the pantheon of the Shakti cult. The Supreme Goddess can be a gentle life-giver as in the case of Lakshmi, Saraswati or Parvati, or as the mistress of death in the form of Durga, Kali and Chamunda. She is a fascinating juxtaposition, both life-perpetuating and potently destructive. In her life-giving form, Shakti can be represented as beautiful, benevolent, maternal, knowledgeable, compassionate and even desirable to the best. She invigorates, cheers and brightens the entire universe. She is represented and described as an idealized woman who is imbued with beauty, virtue and righteousness, and adorned with jewels. In fact, her iconography is drawn from the pre-modern depictions of the salabanjikas, apsaras and surasundaris. In this form, Shakti embraces and enlivens all aspects of reality. As the goddess of destruction and disease, she takes on rather unattractive and repulsive forms. As Sitala Devi Manasa, or Kali, the Devi is shown as haggard, ugly, unkempt and emaciated. However, whatever the form, it is always powerful.

I have dipped into both Puranic and Shakta texts to read the many interpretations and mythologies associated with the iconography, rituals of worship, devotion and representation of the Shakti Peetha as sites of immense power and energy. Each devotee enters the site of the Peetha through their own path of worship, through their respective understanding of the Great

Goddess. The wama panthis or Shakt worshippers, for whom Shakti/Devi is supreme, enter through the tantric path, which is a sectarian movement.

The 51 Peethas have their own singular iconography and their own specific modes of rituals, worship and even prasada, with some standard common offerings like flowers, sweets and vermilion.

RITUALS OF PRAYER AND DARSHAN

While the Shakti Peethas were specific to the body parts of Sati, the rituals of adoration, prayer and worship differed from region to region, given the culture and history of the place. Over time, the Peethas became linked to their respective regions. The local people took ownership of them and started claiming rights over the teerthas and sites. Naturally, the local food and religious and cultural traditions started getting preference over the stated Puranic or standard Sanatan dharmashastras.

In the temples, the daily rituals of worship were similar to the presiding deity, who was normally male, i.e. Vishnu or Shiva, and the feminine was worshipped in the form of their consorts. However, in the Shakti Peethas, the presiding deity was a body part, which while having its own specific service or prayer, was enfolded in the larger narrative of the worship of Shakti in the form of Devi.

The purpose of puja (prayer) is to appease, soothe and mollify the powerful Goddess and embrace the divine energy expressed as life force. The life force itself has many variations, from auspiciousness, health, desire for children, wealth and success, gaining power over intellectual and artistic skill, even victory over enemies. The ritual of puja is heavily invested in darshan. While doing puja, the concept of making eye contact with the deity is the key. Darshan is a two-way concept where the devotee sees the divinity and in turn, the divinity sees the devotee. The concept of darshan crosses all spaces, from intimate puja corners at home in domestic spaces to large public temples including the 51 Shakti Peethas.

The very act of darshan/view is the crucial key that creates the iconic moment where the devotee and the divine are in complete sync. This is the reason why 'Shakt' worshippers make long and arduous journeys to the Shakti Peethas. The idea is to take the energy of the Supreme Goddess while receiving her blessings. The religious rites have three distinct classifications: Nitya, which is daily, normally done at home; Naimittika, which are important days of the deity, and particular festivals (some special to the ishta deva at home or to the presiding deity of the temple); and finally Kamya, which are optional, but a highly desired teertha being one of them.

The ritual of prayer to Shakti is also vested in the panchbhootas, where the five jnanaindriyas, or senses, are included in the aspect of puja:

Panchbhoota	Jnanndriya	Sense	Puja
Akash	Space	Ear	Hear	Pushpam
Vayu	Air	Skin	Touch	Dhoopam
Agni	Fire	Eye	Vision	Lamp
Jal	Water	Tongue	Taste	Water/Ghee
Bhoomi	Earth	Nose	Smell	Chandan

PRASADA

Prasada is both an offering and a blessing. It is offered by the devotee when he/she begins the ritual of puja. In domestic spaces, the devotee performs the puja at an individual, intimate level, often making prasada or an offering of fruits, and a rice and milk pudding with saffron strands and sprinkled with mewa/nuts, particularly almonds and raisins. What I have observed in the offerings by the devotees, is that for Shakti, it is a bali, or animal sacrifice, normally a lamb and sometimes even a buffalo. The very basic prasada for Shakti is meat, alcohol for Bhairava, and a sweet, normally a rice pudding. Since the Shakti Peethas have been appropriated by the devotees of the region, naturally the prasada of the Peetha also acquires a local flavour. In Eastern India, it is primarily khichdi and kheer with poori and potato curry; in South India, it is a variation of the local rice, i.e. pulihora; in Andhra Pradesh, a jaggery laddoo; and in Western India, at the Amba temple in Banaskantha, a delicious sweet made of chickpea flour, the mohanthal, is offered along with sindoor, and makhanas, or dried lotus seeds. In this way, almost every region brings in its regional flavour and speciality as part of the prasada offered at the Shakti Peethas.

Meat as prasada is served in the temple community kitchens only on special occasions when specific sacrifices are conducted.

Holding water in the palm of their hands, or achaman, the devotee asks for forgiveness and blessings before beginning their prayer. In the large public temples, it is the priest who becomes the conduit of devotion and reverence. He is the intermediary who while performing the ritual acts, offers food and flowers to the presiding deity of the temple. Worship in a temple begins by circumambulating the temple and the garbhagriha where the deity lives.

The myth of Sati and the 51 Peethas is an important myth in the worship of the Supreme Goddess. It lays down the template for all those who believe in the Absolute Power of the Mother Goddess, crossing borders from Tantra to Mantra, from *Devi Bhagwat Purana* to *Yogini Hridya Tantra*, right down to the popular Grama Devi in a village to the Kula Devi of a Rajput clan.

SHAKTI AND HER BHAIRAVA

A typical feature in each Shakti Peetha is the presence of a manifestation of Shiva in the form of Bhairava. Sati, whose body parts create the Shakti Peethas, is married to the primordial god, Shiva. However, the Shakti Peethas are completed with a Bhairava shrine within the complex.

In each of the 51 Shakti Peethas, Shiva meditates as Bhairava. Each of the Bhairavas have their own unique iconography and indicators. To understand the cult of Bhairava and the different forms of Bhairavas, it is important to understand the origin, markers, manifestations, representations and expressions of the Bhairavas.

The fierce form of Shiva is Bhairava, who himself has many manifestations. He is even present in Buddhist and Jaina iconographies. In Vajrayana Buddhism, he is known as the Bodhisattva Majushri, Heruka, Vajrabhairava and Yamantaka.

Bhairava is also known as the wandering form of Shiva—the fearful form who is the annihilator. As Mahakaal Bhairava, he is the keeper of time. As Dandapani, he holds a danda/rod to punish the sinners. And as Swaswas, he is one whose mount or vehicle is a dog.

Bhairava moves into the realm of the tantric and with his consort Bhairavi. In this, he is prayed to at midnight during which time, the couple give darshan to their faithful devotees. It is believed that there are 64 Bhairavas, who are divided into eight categories, known as Astabhairavas, the guardians of the eight directions. They are Asithaanga Bhairava, Ruru Bhairava, Chanda Bhairava, Krodha Bhairava, Unmattha Bhairava, Kapaala Bhairava, Bheeshana Bhairava and Samhaara Bhairava.

The Bhairavas are ruled and controlled by the Maha Kaalbhairava, or Kaalbhairava, who as per the Shaivite tantric texts, is also the supreme ruler of the world. In the Trikha system, Bhairava as Para Brahman is also the supreme reality.

Along with Ganesha and Hanuman, the two most popular gods of the Hindu pantheon, the Mother Goddess or Maa is present in every home in the form of the domestic mother herself. I would like to end with a shloka from *Devi Upanishad* where the complement of man and woman in the form of Shiv and Shakti is expressed, which is also the base of the Samkhya Philosophy:

'It is only when Shiva unites with thee, O Shakti, that he becomes the all-powerful Lord. Left to himself, he lacks even the strength to raise his little finger.'

I

Bhabanipur Shakti Peetha
Karatoya, Bhabanipur, Bangladesh

*Sarva mangal mangalayee, shiva sarvadha sadhike,
sharan-ye triambikae Gauri, Narayani Namostute*

[Salutations to you, O Narayani, who is the auspiciousness in all the auspicious, auspiciousness herself. Complete with all the auspicious attributes, and who fulfills all the objectives of the devotees (purusharthas—dharma, artha, kama and moksha), who is the giver of refuge, with three eyes and a shining face; salutations to you, O Narayani.]

The greenest jewel of Asia and a country that is woven through with more than 700 rivers, the lush landscape of Bangladesh has been for long a tantalising escape for adventurers and travellers alike. Bangla culture has its unique way of slowing you down to its own rhythmic beat, as you traverse its scenic beauty by land, boat, or the rich cultural threads. It is in the liveliness of this country that the Maa Bhabani or Aparna Peetha is found, in the Bhabanipur Shrine. Maa Bhabani is one of the most powerful forms of Durga or Adi Shakti, and here she is also called Aparna Devi. It is believed that after Devi Sati's self-immolation, when Shri Vishnu took the Sudarshan

Chakra to her body, her left anklet fell on the hallowed grounds of Karatoya in Bangladesh; the Bhairava that protects her here is called Vaman, an embodiment of Lord Shiva. Etymologically speaking, Bhavani is Tara. She is the one who rules the universe, the ultimate Mother of Creation. As Aparna, she is the Devi who is dedicated to Lord Shiva, one so devoted to her lord that even the falling leaves go unnoticed by her. As the story goes, when Devi Parvati was performing her penance to be united with Lord Shiva, so severe and devoted were her austerities that she survived only on a single leaf for nutrition, begetting the name 'Aparna'. At this Shakti Peetha, she is worshipped as a ferocious form of Durga, and the idol which lies in the inner sanctum of the temple is that of Mahakali.

The Karatoya Bhabanipur Shakti Peetha is located in the village Bogura, in the hamlet of Sherpur Thana. The shrine itself is a mere 28 km from Sherpur. There are many ways of reaching Bhabanipur, but most visitors make use of the well-connected public transport system such as the bus service which runs from Natore via Nulkamod and Chandaikona. The shrine itself is sanctified with the flowing water of River Karatoya, revered as the Ganga. Devotees visiting the Shakti Peetha take dips in the holy water ridding themselves of the darkness of the ego. If the local lore is to be believed, the Karatoya Bhabani Shakti Peetha has the power to heal all skin-related ailments, and the Goddess here is known for her healer's touch.

The 4 acres of the temple complex have become something of a conclave of the sanctified. Going beyond the main shrine, one finds the Patal Bhairava temple, the protector of the Peetha, the Gopal temple, the Basudev temple, and the Nat or Atchala temple, all of which have varying associations with Lord Shiva. The Shakha Pukur, a holy pond in Bhabhanipur village, was considered as the site of the Shakti Peetha. This temple had been demolished by the Combined Forces of Bangladesh as an unauthorised structure but later rescued by the Bhabhanipur

Temple Renovation Development and Management Committee which took on the massive task of the renovation and the maintenance of the temple. This is perhaps the reason why one does not find an idol of Aparna Devi, and instead the image of Mahakali is the centre of worship.

According to legend, the King of Natore and his grandson, the Maharaja Ramkrishna, used to meditate near this temple; the tranquil ambience, the resonating spiritual energy facilitated the mastering of Siddhis. There is a beautiful story, a part of the local lore, that tells us how the Shakha Pukur, the pond of conch bangles, got its name: a poor seller of glass or conch bangles once came across a little girl, or kanya, not too far off from the shrine. Her face showed divine charm and there was liveliness in her eyes that seemed to know more than was normal for someone so young. Decked in red, she wore a red tilak, beautiful jewels, and an easy smile on her face. The kanya asked the bangle-seller for some bangles and as payment she asked him to collect the money from Rajbari, since she was the daughter of the Maharaja of Natore. When the bangle-seller went to the Rajbari, that is the Maharaja's court, nobody seemed to know who this girl was. When the Queen of Bhabhanipur, Rani Bhawani, heard about this incident, she was intrigued enough to seek out the girl. She went back to the very same spot where the poor bangle-seller had first encountered the child, but she found no one. All of a sudden it dawned on the Queen that the girl was the Goddess Bhabani herself, in her kanya form, and as the Queen prayed for the Goddess to reveal herself, she emerged from the depths of the pond, giving her darshan—her arms filled with glass bangles, one hand in the mudra blessing all who worship her.

Navratri is celebrated here with special pujas and yagnas. Deepavali and Ram Navami are equally popular. In the days of the festivities, the deities are bathed and dressed in all their fineries in the morning and the Balyo Bhog is offered to the divinity. In the afternoon, the Anna Bhog is offered to the divinity, and in the evening after the aarti, prasada is distributed among all those who come visiting. Among other celebrations there is notably the mela or fair which is held within the temple complex through the month of Baisakh according to the Bengali calendar. Additionally every year on the auspicious eve of Magh Purnima and Ram Navami, two of the most important festivals celebrated at the Bhabhanipur Shakti Peetha, visitors from all across Bangladesh arrive in hoards to receive darshan from the great Goddess, the mother of the universe, or Adi Shakti herself. A quick dip in the water begins the puja rituals in the early hours of the morning, followed by morning aarti and bhog. It is believed that those who come to the Goddess with the purity and the unsullied innocence of her kanya form in their hearts, find all their wishes granted by the benevolent mother.

2

Avanti Shakti Peetha
Bhairava Parvat, Ujjain, Madhya Pradesh

Ujjainyam Maha Kali, Peethikayam Puruhutika
Odhyane Girija Devi, Manikya Daksha Vatike

[Goddess Mahakali in Ujjain Puruhutika in Peethika, that is her Peetha, Goddess Girija in Odhyana and Goddess Manikya in the house of Daksha.]

Nestled in the heart of India, the ancient city of Ujjain in the central state of India—Madhya Pradesh—is one of the important Shakti Peethas. It has attracted one and all, be it tourists, traders or pilgrims, with the undeniable lure of its spiritual energy pulsing through the sacred sites dotted along its geography. In ancient times, it was known as Ujjayini and in the epic Mahabharata, it was mentioned as the capital of the Avanti Kingdom. Since the 4th century BCE, it has been the prime meridian for Hindu geographers and scholars. It is most widely known in the form of a spiritual abode for Hinduism. Ujjain is one of the Sapta Puri, one among the seven sacred cities of India, which is why it is one of the four cities that hosts the larger-than-life Kumbh Mela, the pilgrimage festival hosted once every 12 years. At any time of the year, one has to jostle along its busy river ghats, elbow to elbow, with countless devotees as they make their offerings in the various famous temples of Ujjain. As one loses their way in the maze of alleyways, they can be almost certain to end up at the their spiritual epicentre.

In this most hallowed of cities is the Avanti Shakti Peetha, widely known here as Shri Mahakali, protected by Lord Shiva's Bhairava form, Lambakarna, which literally means 'the long-eared'. According to mythology, after the self-immolation of Sati at Prajapati Daksha's yagna, it was in this holy spot that Devi Sati's upper lip fell, and it is also believed by many as one of the seven places on Earth where one can find sublime release from the suffering of life through moksha, or enlightenment.

The Avanti Shakti Peetha has a truly unique location atop the rocky climbs of the Bhairava Parvat, which stands tall on the banks of the river Shipra in Ujjain. It is believed to be nearly 5,000 years old and to have weathered the ages, changing dynasties, rules and the yugas. This ancient Peetha is one among the Ashtadasa Peetha which make up the 18 primary Shakti Peethas venerated in the Shakta tradition as mentioned in Adi Sankaracharya's *Ashtadasha Shakti Peetha Strotam*. Adi Sankaracharya was considered to be one of the noblest and most learned theologians in the 8th century. A stalwart of the Bhakti movement, among his many strotams he had composed one dedicated to Adi Shakti and her 18 forms which were embodied by her 18 Shakti Peethas. These Peethas became the Ashtadasa. When Avanti Maa is worshipped as Mahakalika here, she becomes part of the divine feminine trinity or the Tri-Devi—Mahasaraswati, Mahalakshmi and Mahakalika. In close quarters is the Mahakaleshwar Jyotirlingam, one of the 12 Jyotirlingams, and if legend is to be believed the temple city is where Sri Krishna, Sudama and Balarama received their education from Maharishi Sandipani.

The structure of the temple of Mata Avanti in itself is beautifully framed within the natural environs of Bhairava Parvat, with a stony pedantic form made using uniquely colourful stones all around its interiors and walls. In fact, the wall and the roof of the temple are made of magnificently inscribed stones offering a picturesque view of the city of Ujjain to all visiting devotees and tourists. The idol of the Devi that is placed within the sanctum sanctorum is kept covered in a red garment, and the tongue of Devi Avanti's idol is stretched bare to the world. As the daily prayers are performed and the crowds move in unison for their darshan, one can hope to experience the fierce energy that emanates from the shrine in all its potency—for Mahakali is the warrior Adi Shakti, the destroyer of the ego.

Interestingly enough, there are no official records pointing to the exact time period when this temple was constructed or who constructed this temple, but what is abundantly clear is that the temple received its name from the Avanti Kingdom mentioned in the Mahabharata as the Avanti Devi Peetha. There is a beautiful but brief description in the epic poem of the Avanti Devi temple calling it the prime place of worship of the inhabitants of the city of Ujjayini.

The Avanti Maa or Mahakali, the Adi Shakti form of this Peetha, is said to be the fierce protector of this city and her people. According to the legend of Kali, there was once a demon named Andhakaleshwar who wreaked havoc across the three worlds. No one was able to stop nor contain him since he had a boon from Lord Brahma himself that wherever his blood would fall, in that very spot more demons, more Andhakaleshwars, would be born. In order to protect the world, Adi Parashakti took the form of Mahakali and during the fierce battle fought between the Goddess and the demon, Mahakali spread her tongue and drank all the blood that flowed from the demon, thus killing him.

Another quaint tale about the Avanti Shakti Peetha is that this is the place where the great poet Kalidasa received his knowledge by the grace of Mahakali. The Goddess had inscribed all the texts and the poetry that Kalidasa was to ever compose, upon his tongue, as he visited her with devotion in his heart and a prayer for knowledge.

Devi Avanti and the Bhairava Lambakarna are the manifestations of the divine energy that combine to form the life-force of the universe, as Adi Shakti and Shiva fuse together to maintain balance in the cosmos. Avanti Maa as the 'modest' and Lambakarna as the 'long-eared one', together bestow the goodwill of the universe upon their devotees by bringing an end to the illusion of the ego. Incidentally, Lambakarna is another name for Shiva and Parvati's son Ganesha.

Ujjain comes alive during the sacred Kumbh Mela, drawing devout pilgrims and visitors from all over India and the world to the tune of nearly 75 million people. The revelry of these festivities take over all the sacred sites of the city including Bhairava Parvat where there is constant worship and vigil kept for the Goddess. Additionally, Shivratri, the day of Shiva and Parvati's union, is marked by a special puja held for married women, who come to pay their respects to Avanti Devi.

3

Bahula Shakti Peetha
Ketugram, Katwa, West Bengal

Bahulaayaam Vaama-Baahur-Bahula-
[A]akhyaa Ca Devataa |
Bhiiruko Bhairavas-Tatra Sarva-Siddhi-
Pradaayakah ||15||

[At Bahula, my mama bah, or left arm fell, and there the Devata, implied the Devi, is known as Bahula, meaning the creator of abundance. There, the Bhairava is called as Bhiruka, meaning the creator of fear. The Devi, Adi Shakti, is the giver of all Siddhis, or spiritual accomplishments.]

Kali presides over the capital city of West Bengal, Kolkata, named after the manifestation of the Devi as Kali. Kolkata is the home to the Great Goddess herself. Deep in the Shakta circuit of West Bengal one finds the benevolent Bahula Devi at Ketugram, near Katwa. This is one of the benevolent forms of the divine Maa, Adi Shakti. She is the bestower of all spiritual knowledge, the answer that all who seek are in search of. Interestingly, her Bhairava or consort Bhiruka is the creator of fear itself. Together they are a reflection of the nature of knowledge itself, which is that only beyond fear can one find the answers that one is in search of.

It was said that when Lord Vishnu, donning the role of the preserver, had used his Sudarshan Chakra on the burnt corpse of Devi Sati in order to protect the world from the destruction caused by Shiva's dance of destruction, the Tandava, Maa Sati's left arm had fallen in Ketugram. 'Bahu' in Sanskrit means arm, and 'Bahula' means lavish. It refers to the prosperity that the Goddess Bahula brings, as if to carry out these boons by her very arm. Bahula and the Bhairava, Bhiruka, are the very manifestations of Shiv and Adi Shakti. In fact 'Bhiruka' also means one who has attained the highest levels of meditation or the sarvasiddhayak, which once again embodies his role as the protector of the Peetha that bestows upon its devotees all manner of boons.

Such is the veneration that Bahula Shakti Peetha inspires, devotees are known to never have left this benevolent goddess' shrine empty-handed. She is truly the guarantor of wishes as long as those who approach her do so with a genuine heart of bhakti or devotion and a longing for true salvation. Miracle stories are part of the treasure trove of this Peetha.

It is by the banks of River Ajay that the edifice of Bahula Devi stands tall at Ketugram. The aura of reposeful meditation reaches far into the surrounding areas of this Peetha, enveloping visitors in its blissful embrace. Within the temple complex is an enlarged courtyard right before the garbhagriha, the sanctum sanctorum or the innermost sanctuary of the Devi. The vast open space is crowded by the visiting devotees and despite the crowds, one can actually experience the magnetic pull towards the Peetha; a longing, it would seem, for Adi Shakti's darshan. The openness of the temple's plan makes it essential for all who visit to come prepared for high temperatures, which often rises depending on the month to more than 40°C, which is why the popular seasons are the cooler winter months. The flooring of the temple is built with red stones so as to ensure that the indoors remain comfortably cool even in the harshest of summers. The distinct location of this shrine, which is both remote yet not too isolated, endows upon it a serenity. One can hear the chiming of the bells and the chanting of the Devi's mantras even from a distance.

The idol of the Goddess Bahula Devi in this Shakti Peetha is gentler than her other incarnates, seen as she is accompanied by her two sons Kartikeya and Ganesha in the form of the mother. Lord Kartikeya, the god of war, here is also the god of fertility, and Lord Ganesha epitomizes all that is auspicious in the world, removing whatever hurdles may arise so as to ensure a smooth journey onwards.

In the vicinity of this Shakti Peetha is a conclave of significant temples such as the Kankaleshwari Kali Mandir. The idol in this temple is made in the form of the human skeleton along with the prominent depiction of nerves and muscle on a black basalt stone. At some distance is also the Sarvamangala shrine which shows the mighty Durga aloft her lion, her 18 arms outstretched, as she marches on as Mahishasuraa Mardini. Not too far is the Shiva lingam temple dedicated to Lord Shiva, completing the union of the two.

There is a long-standing tradition of Nitya Puja or the daily meeting with god in this Peetha. It is the ultimate celebration of Bhakti as it creates a consistent experience of devotion and adoration. The Nitya Puja is offered to the entire Shiva Parivar which is the Devi, Lord Shiva, Lord Kartikeya and Lord Ganesha in the auspicious of hours of dawn. Devotees make the offerings of fruits and sweets to the Goddess as the temple priest perform the morning aarti. The Sandhya Bhog later in the evening is then culminated with the lighting of oil lamps, aarti and the distribution of prasada.

Maha Shivratri, the eternal night of Shiva and Parvati, is celebrated with much gusto in Bahula Peetha. Devotees fast all day and all night, offering fruits, milk and Bilva patra (leaves) to the idol of Lord Shiva. All through the night one can hear the bhajans sung in praise of the divine couple, Shiva and Parvati. However, it is the pomp and splendour of Durga Puja which outshines all revelry at Bahula Devi. West Bengal is known for its Durga Puja celebration, through the nine days of Navratri, worshipping the nine forms of Adi Shakti. At Bahula, these celebrations gain much fervor and delight with special yagnas and pujas conducted in honour of both Durga and her fiercer form, Kali. As visitors gather to worship the Divine Mother, they fast for the nine days of Navratri, their dhyan single-mindedly on the Devi; only after the evening Puja is completed and the bhog given to the Goddess do they break their fast. It is believed by some that it is the intensity of this devotion that rids one of the ego and as such bestows upon them the blessings of the Divine Mother, who provides the passage away from the trappings of the material world.

4

Triambakeshwar Bhramari Devi Shakti Peetha

Panchvati, Nasik, Maharashtra

*Namah sivabhyam navayauvanabhyam
Parasparaslistavapurdharabhyam
Nagendrakanyavrsaketanabhyam
Namo namah sankaraparvatibhyam*

[Obeisance to Siva and Sivaa (Uma), the eternally young pair who hold each other's body in mutual embrace.
I offer again and again my obeisance to Sankara and Parvati, the one with the bull for his banner and the other, the beloved daughter of the king of mountains (Himavan).]

—UMAMAHESVARA STOTRAM[1]

Twenty-four kilometres away from Nasik in Maharashtra, in the western coast of India, is the holy city of Triambakeshwar, which holds within its sacred geography two powerful energies—that of Shiva and Shakti. It is also one of the four holy cities to host the Kumbh Mela once every 12 years. It is here that the Peetha of Bhramari Devi is

---

[1] https://stotranidhi.com/en/uma-maheshwara-stotram-in-english/

located. It is believed that Sati's chin fell here. The Shakti Peetha is thus known as the Bhramari Peetha.

Adi Shakti, in this most famed Peetha, has many names that point to its popularity. Some of them are Chibuka or the one with the chin; with Shiva, she is called Sarvasiddhish or the one who bestows all desires; and she is also the Devi Saptashrungi or the goddess with seven arms. According to legend, Goddess Saptashrungi Nivasini dwells in her hilly abode of seven peaks ('sapta' meaning seven and 'shrungi' meaning peaks) in the village Sani, which is at some distance from Nasik.

Bhramari Devi, the form of Adi Shakti, who embodies this Peetha, is a dark-skinned goddess and is considered to be another form of Mahakali, the literal meaning of her name being 'the form of a bee'. She is described in the *Devi Bhagvatam* 'as brilliant as a million dark suns', and is surrounded by a retinue of black bees who she holds back by her fist. She destroys the egoistic demons of ignorance, illusion and folly, as her bees make the sound that becomes her Beejakshar mantra or Seed-Mantra, Hring.

If one were to follow the local lore surrounding this Shakti Peetha, it is said that the Devi was swayambhu, that is self-manifested, on a rock in one of the seven peaks of Vani. Her idol here is magnificent in its height, a good ten feet tall. Bhramari Devi has 18 hands which hold weapons of war, presenting a truly fierce and empowered image of an otherwise benevolent Divine Mother. She holds the battle axe, mace, arrow, thunderbolt, bow, cudgel, lance, sword, shield, trident, noose, spinning disc, necklace of prayer beads or rudra mala, lotus, water pot, conch, bell and cup. While one hand reigns over her bees, two more are folded in the mudras which grant boons to the pious and remove all fears from the heart of her devotees. The idol is perennially coated in the vermilion hue of sindoor, which is a symbol of the married woman, and a signifier of the power of the grihani or the housewife. The sindoor is also considered exceedingly auspicious in the region and is often given out as prasada.

Bhramari Devi is also known by many as Mahishasuraa Mardini, or the slayer of the demon Mahishasuraa, who took the form of a buffalo. This is perhaps why at the foot of the hill of this Shakti Peetha, right where one begins climbing the stairs towards the shrine, there is a buffalo's head made of stone, as if to forever lie at the feet of the great Goddess—a trophy of her conquest over ignorance.

In the epic poem of Ramayana, there is mention of the Dandakarnya forest which is part of the Saptashrungi mountains. This most auspicious forest with all the markings of the bounty of nature was where Lord Rama and Devi Sita worshipped the benevolent Goddess Amba, a maternal form of Shakti. As a legend of Bhramari Devi goes, there was once a daitya called Aruna, who wanted to defeat all the devas. He had meditated to Lord Brahma for thousands of years and after completing many severe austerities, Lord Brahma, pleased by his devotion, appeared before him to grant him the boon of his tapasya. Aruna was well prepared for this moment. He had imagined time and again the cleverly constructed manner in which he would ask for his heart's desire, which was immortality, widely known as the one boon the gods do not grant. Aruna asked Brahma Dev that no god, weapon, man, woman, two-legged or four-legged creature should be able to kill him. Brahma, having begun the cycle of karma, had to grant his devotee his wish for it wasn't exactly immortality that he had asked for. The moment Lord Brahma said, '*Tatahastu*,' the demon prepared for war against the devas with his enormous rakshasa army.

The gods, left with no viable repose, sought the benevolent Mother of the Universe or Adi Shakti for help in conquering the rakshasa army. When the Goddess appeared to help the devas, she arrived in a swarm of black bees, which enveloped her body, whispering her Beeja mantra. They attacked the demon, bringing an end to the terrifying havoc that he had created. It is in this incarnation that she came to be known as Bhramari Devi or the goddess of bees.

Interestingly enough, in the orbit of most Shakti Peethas, one often finds temples and shrines dedicated to other forms of the Devi and her respective consorts. Located on the western side door of the Kalaram temple near Panchavati is the Sita Gufaa or Sita's Cave, which can be accessed only by a narrow passage. There is a Shiva lingam here which, according to local lore, was worshipped by Shri Rama, Shri Lakshman and Devi Sita during their exile and when Lakshman lay injured and unconscious on the battlefield in Lanka, Hanuman came to the Saptashringi to bring back the Sanjeevani booti that had life-giving properties.

As part of the worship of the Devi, her idol is given its abhishekam or daily bath after which the Goddess is dressed in new clothes, adorned with precious jewels like necklaces, silver nose rings, floral wreaths, etc. There are special pujas held on Tuesdays and Fridays, Navami, Ashtami and Chaturdashis of each month. These days are considered extremely auspicious in the Bhramari Devi Shakti Peetha, with visitors coming in hoards regularly for the darshan of their beloved Mata. The festivals of Navratri and Durga Puja are celebrated with a mesmerising display of cheer and bhakti and there is an important festival that is celebrated in particular in this Shakti Peetha where childless women pray for the boon of a child. Held mostly in the Chaitra month, which begins on Ramnavami and ends on Chaitra Poornima, during this festival the Goddess is given a Panchamruta snan and on the final day the deity is taken through the village in the presence of the village head, the banner of the Goddess hoisted on the hilltop for everyone to have darshan. Many believe that one never remains empty-handed after praying to the Goddess and so this tradition has remained in place since as far back as the 15th century.

5

Brajeshwari Devi Shakti Peetha
Kangra, Himachal Pradesh

Ya devi sarva bhuteshu, shanti rupena sangsthita
Ya devi sarva bhuteshu, shakti rupena sangsthita
Ya devi sarva bhuteshu, matri rupena sangsthita
Yaa devi sarva bhuteshu, buddhi rupena sangsthita
Namastasyai, namastasyai, namastasyai, namo namaha

[The goddess who is omnipresent as the personification of universal mother, the goddess who is omnipresent as the embodiment of power, the goddess who is omnipresent as the symbol of peace, O Goddess who resides everywhere in all living beings as intelligence and beauty, I bow to her, I bow to her, I bow to her again and again.]

—DEVI MAHATAMYA STOTRAM[2]

One of the favourites abodes of the Great Goddess is the mountainous terrain of the Kangra district of Himachal Pradesh, a part of Trigarta. The area between the ancient river Shatadroo (known as Sutlej today) and River Ravi, and surrounded by the Shivaliks and the Dhauladhars, is

---

[2] https://sanskritdocuments.org/doc_Devii/devImAhAtmyastotram.html?lang=sa

the Brajeshwari Devi Shakti Peetha.

According to the epic poem Mahabharata, the Brajeshwari Shakti Peetha temple was built by the Pandavas who not only worshipped the Devi in her Durga aspect but were also given the Kingdom of Nagarkot by Dhritrashtra in an attempt at fairness. The legend says that one day the Pandavas each dreamt of the Devi and in their dream she told them that she is situated in the Nagarkot village and if they wanted to secure themselves, they should build a temple for her in Nagarkot to protect themselves from the destruction of their circumstances or destiny. Not long after the dream, the magnificent temple of the Devi was built in the Nagarkot village.

This temple did not however have an easy history. It was looted multiple times by Muslim invaders who entered the subcontinent from the northwest frontiers. It is believed that Mohammad Ghazni looted this temple at least five times. It was a storehouse of tonnes and tonnes of gold, the temple bells were made of pure silver and the Devi herself wore jewels and ornaments of the finest materials and studded with rare gems. In the year 1905, the temple was finally destroyed by a massive powerful earthquake and subsequently the government embarked on an attempt to rebuild the structure with a stronger, more pervading foundation.

Much of the original look has been retained, the main gate, which is the entrance into the temple, has a Nagar khanna or drum house and is built like a Bassein fortress with a strong entrance. The temple is surrounded by a stone wall which is in continuation of its fort-like exterior. Entering the temple complex, one finds the main area where Brajeshwari Devi is present in the form of her Pindi or stone form. The temple also has a Bhairava temple smaller than the Devi's but present beside hers. In front of the temple of the Goddess is an idol of Dhyanu Bhagat, who had offered his head to the Goddess during Akbar's rule, beseeching her to protect them. He is forever

Brajeshwari Temple
Photo: Creative Commons/Varun Shiv Kapur

commemorated here in the embrace of the Divine Mother.

Among the many celebrations at the temple is the festival of Makar Sakranti, which comes in the second week of January. The legend of the Devi is that after killing the demon Mahishasura in battle, the Devi had been injured. To heal those injuries, the Goddess applied healing butter in Nagarkot. To this day in reverence of the Devi, her Pindi is covered with butter and the festival is celebrated all week long in the temple.

The Brajeshwari Devi Shakti Peetha is directly across the temple of Vaidyanath. Both these temples are connected by a red-coloured silk rope. The belief is that those couples who bind the two tops of the temples with silk threads will have a happy married and familial life, blessed as they will be by Lord Shiva and Devi Parvati themselves.

The temple itself is not as grand as it was in the days of the yore, however it is still a beautiful sight. The idols of Durga and Parvati are in the form of a rock, and devotees who come visiting climb up to offer flowers and milk to the Goddess. The offerings can also be given to the Pindi in the inner sanctum of the temple. In the temple campus itself, many forms of Shakti are found surrounding the Vaidyanath temple, such as Kali, Tara, Banglamukhi, Sandhya, Saraswati, Annapurna and Jagatjanani, who are among the most significant ones. The locals worship the Devi in each of her forms with special mantras and strotams.

In the months of Shravan around July and the month of Magh in February, the festivals are primarily conducted in Vaidyanath and the Devi's temple, commemorating their story. Ashviyuja Navratri in October is also conducted here since Vaidyanath is a Siddhapeetha where sadhus and yogis come to attain various siddhis. In fact, many tantrics worship Brajeshwari Devi to attain her blessing on their path to enlightenment. The Jagatmata here is worshipped in both her forms of benevolence and fearsomeness as Tripura Sundari or Tripura Bhairavi, and

Chhinnamasta. As Tripura Sundari, she is worshipped alongside Ganesha as her Rishi, and as Chhinnamasta she is worshipped along with Ravanasura as her Rishi.

6

Chhinnamastika Devi Shakti Peetha
Chintpurni, Una District, Himachal Pradesh

Chintpurni is a town in Una district of Himachal Pradesh. It is named after Goddess Chhinnamastika and it is here that one of the Devi's most prominent Shakti Peethas reside. Nestled within the western Himalayan range in the north and the Shivalik in the east, on the border of the flourishing state of Punjab, one finds themselves in the idyllic hamlet of Chintpurni, literally meaning 'she who fulfils one's wishes'. This Shakti Peetha is believed to be the place where a part of the Devi's foot fell, sliced by Lord Vishnu's Sudarshan Chakra.

The Chhinnamastika Devi is one of the Dus Mahavidyas, a group of goddesses worshipped in the Hindu faith as representations of the ten great revelations of spiritual enlightenment. As the story goes, when Devi Sati wanted to attend her father Prajapati Daksha's havan kund to disrupt it in retaliation of the slight he had caused her husband, one of the Tridevs, by not inviting him, Lord Shiva forbade her, knowing fully well the consequences of such a visit. The Devi, not pleased with the refusal, transformed herself into the Dus Mahavidyas or her ten transcendental forms. When Lord Shiva found himself surrounded by the fierce forms of the goddess's spiritual knowledge, frightened by her intensity he gave her permission to go. These forms were Kali, Tara, Tripura Sundari, Bhuvaneshwari, Chhinnamasta, Bhairavi, Dhumamati, Banglamukhi, Matangi and Kamala.

Chhinnamasta, Chhinnamastika or Prachanda Chandika, as a goddess of the esoteric tradition, represents the dual nature of life and death. She is both the fierce form of the Devi, as well as her gentler life-giving aspect. In her depictions she is shown as a decapitated goddess who stands in the nude upon a divine copulating couple, with her own severed head in one hand and a scimitar in the other. Three jet streams of blood spurt from her bleeding neck, which are drunk by her two attendants Jaya and Vijaya, and the third stream by the Goddess herself. It is because of this imagery that Chhinnamasta is known as the severed-headed one and is considered to be a goddess of contradictions. On one hand, she symbolises sexual self-control and is the embodiment of sexual energy and the gift of it, but she also represents the temporality of death, destruction, life and recreation. The Goddess is the conveyor of a form of spiritual realization and the awakening of Kundalini energy within us that celebrates the duality of everything in the universe. It is as if to say that enlightenment comes from the dual nature of the universe itself.

As per the legends surrounding Goddess Chhinnamasta, there is a particular emphasis on self-sacrifice in her worship and in her sect. This form of self-sacrifice though has a maternal element or instinct driving it forth, in that there is a greater collective interest in the sacrifice that she demands or stands for. According to an account in *Pranatosini Tantra*, describing the origin of the Goddess, once Goddess Parvati had gone bathing with her two attendants Jaya and Vijaya, also known in tantric traditions as Dakini and Varini. The two women became hungry at some point and asked Devi Parvati to provide them with nourishment and something to eat. The Devi told them to wait and that they could eat once they were home.

However in some time the attendants again begged the Goddess to satisfy their hunger. The merciful Goddess as the Mother of the Universe, severed her own head with the edges of her fingernails and through the blood that was released from within her, she nourished her attendants. Henceforth, she was known as Chhinnamasta and the story became symbolic of maternal self-sacrifice; the interesting alternative of blood instead of milk is considered to point towards the nourishment symbolized in the renewal of the universe.

In another more fearsome legend, after defeating the demons Shumbh and Nishumbh, Goddess Parvati and her aides Jaya and Vijaya went to bathe themselves. Jaya and Vijaya were still taken over by the madness of war, and asked the Goddess to quench their thirst. The Devi, ever so merciful, decapitated her own head, and the three streams of blood which spurted out were consumed by her two sahyoginis and herself, nourishing and satisfying their hunger for war and destruction.

This Shakti Peetha in its picturesque surroundings amidst the highest peaks of the Sola Singhi mountain range is connected by well-trodden roads as a popular destination for travellers—tourists, pilgrims and sadhus alike. There are plenty of dharamshalas surrounding the temple as part of a network of pilgrim destinations. Not too far away one finds Thaneek Pura, Sheetala Devi temple, Chamunda Devi temple, Jwalaji temple, etc. Maa Chhinnamasta is uniquely worshipped by both householders and sadhus of the tantric tradition. She symbolizes the separation of the mind from the body, and its submission to the vast spiritual consciousness that is part of the greater divine energy. As the headless Goddess of transcendental knowledge, you enter her abode through the depth of the mind, uncovered only through meditation and sadhna.

The temple itself is within a huge complex that is simplistic in its architecture. Situated in the middle of the complex is the temple's garbhagriha, or the innermost sanctum. This sanctum

Chintpurni Temple
Photo: Creative Commons/Guptaele

houses the images of the Devi or the Mother Goddess and in this Shakti Peetha she is worshipped in the form of a pindi or round stone that is said to symbolize her feet. The beloved Goddess here is also known as Maa Chandi, and it is believed that she is protected on all four sides by her husband and consort Lord Shiva. This belief is re-affirmed by the pilgrim circuit that has been created in modern times, which includes a visit to Narayana Mahadeva in the west, Kaleshwar Mahadeva in the east, Muchkund Mahadeva in the south, and Shiva Bari in the north. The union of the Shiva temple and the Devi temple in the geography of Chintpurni is meant to be representative of the divine unity of Shiva-Shakti in the Ardhanareshwar form. Additionally, the Bhairava accompanying and attached to the Chhinnamasta Peetha is called Rudra Mahadev, another fierce form of Shiva and he along with the Devi, provides safe passage towards a divine union by protecting the spiritual consciousness of all devotees that come visiting.

During the months of Navratras, the temple observes grand fairs and festivities which turn into a place of gathering with people from all over the country flocking to receive the blessings of the Goddess. The fair is held near the premises of the Goddess Bhagwati Chhinnamsatika temple and is held thrice a year in the months of March–April, July–August and September–October. In the months of July and August, celebrations take place as part of the 10-day period of the Shukla Paksha, a time considered as immensely auspicious to the Goddess. On the eighth day, the reverence and worship of the Goddess rises to its zenith as she is celebrated as the destroyer of all evil, her grace and power embodied by her devotees.

7

Dakshayani Devi Shakti Peetha
Manas, Tibet

Maanase Dakssa-Hasto Me Devii Daakssaayannii Hara |
Amaro Bhairavas-Tatra Sarva-Siddhi-Pradaayakah ||12||

[At Manasa, my daksha hasta, or right hand, fell. The Devi there is known as Dakshayani (literally meaning the daughter of Daksha). This is where Amara is the Bhairava (literally meaning immortal). The Devi there is the giver of all Siddhis, or spiritual accomplishments.]

One of the holiest places in the world is the Mansa Devi Peetha, as the Devi here is also the bestower of the fulfillment of every devotee's desires. This Peetha is located in one of the most sanctimonious locales, beside the sacred waters of the Lake Mansarovar. The Goddess here is a form of Adi Shakti known as Mansa and her Bhairava, or the form of Shiva her consort, is Lord Amar. According to the mythology of the Devi, this is the spot where the Goddess's right hand fell.

While the site is a draw for all devotees of the Goddess, it is of specific import to the Shakta sect of Hinduism or the followers of the Devi. *Vishnu Purana* tells us of Mount Kailash which is the Axis Mundi of the world (the point of connection between the physical world and spiritual world). According to the Puranic texts, the four sides of its peak are made up of crystal, ruby, gold and lapis lazuli. A visit to Mount Kailash is considered a most sacred pilgrimage, since it is the source of all the holy rivers such as Indus, Brahmaputra, Ganga, Yamuna and Sutlej. The Mansa Devi Shakti Peetha is at the gateway of this journey, since Kailash Parvat is also considered to be the abode of Lord Shiva and Devi Parvati.

The ancient scriptures mention that those who take a dip in the holy waters of the Mansarovar Lake followed by the circumambulation of the Mount Kailash peak, are absolved of all their sins for generations to come and attain salvation. The lake is also considered to have legendary healing powers, and is considered to be the resting place of Hamsa, the swan belonging to Lord Brahma, one of the holy trinity. While there is no actual temple built here to offer prayers at, there is a big boulder which is the object of worship as a symbol of Devi Parvati.

The temple itself is situated a little way away in the village known as Shard or Sharada where the two rivers, Jhelum and Kishnaganga, flow from Kashmir to meet one another. To reach the temple one has to go via Bandipur in North Kashmir, about 80 km from Srinagar. It is very close to Pakistan-occupied Kashmir, so the security is high. However one does get glimpses of some of the most scenic sights in the country. The temple itself is ancient. It has four doors in all four directions, but the main entrance is from the west. There is a stairway leading to the main entrance, and it is notable how plain the construction of the temple itself is. The innermost sanctum is where the prayers are offered to the Devi daily. There are 63 stairs leading to it and one feels truly elevated during the darshan of this rectangular abode of the Goddess. Speaking of the architecture of the temple, one can't help but notice the expansive courtyard and open nature of the entire structure, with pillars and columns, which characterize the typical Kashmiri style of design.

As part of the rituals of the temple, devotees visiting offer cow's milk and agricultural produce such as wheat, rice, fruits and cereals like barley to the Devi. A fair is held in the month of Badrapada Masa, the months of August–September, on the eighth day of the Shukla Paksha Ashtami. On this day, thousands of devotees fill the temple seeking a darshan from the Goddess in a beautiful scene of deep veneration and devoted love.

8

Gandaki Devi Shakti Peetha
Muktinath, Nepal

*Gannddakyaam Ganndda-Paatan-Ca Tatra
Siddhir-Na Samshayah |
Tatra Saa Gannddakii Cannddii Cakrapaannis-Tu
Bhairavah ||14||*

[At Gandaki, my ganda, or cheek, fell, and in that place there is no doubt about the attainment of Siddhi, also known as spiritual accomplishment. There, the Devi is known as Gandaki Chandi, the literal meaning of which is 'Chandi at Gandaki'.
The Bhairava here is known as Chakrapani, which means 'the one with a disc in hand'.]

Among the flutter of the prayer flags in Nepal is a refined pace that can only be found beside a Himalayan viewpoint. As one strolls through the market squares past the busy hum of the medieval cities of Kathmandu, Patan and Bhaktapur, there lies a confluence of spirituality—Buddhism, Shaivism, Vaishnavism and Shaktism. Nepal is home to temples, century-old stupas and Buddhist monasteries. Even after the 2015 earthquake, the country remains a cultural conglomerate of deep-rooted spirituality. Nepal, the only

Hindu kingdom of the world, has long celebrated the Devi. The Divine Goddess, the Kanya Mata or Kumari, is home to the Gandaki Devi Shakti Peetha.

Legend has it that Muktinath is where Devi Sati's right cheek had fallen and thus it is here that she is worshipped as Gandaki Chandi or the one who overcomes all obstacles. Her Bhairava is called Chakrapani or the one who holds the disc. The Gandaki which babbles close to the Muktinath temple is considered to be precious to Goddess Adi Shakti; the water is believed to have holy properties. According to local lore, the shaligram stones or fossil stones which are found in the great depths of Gandaki are considered to be a boon from the great Goddess herself. Interestingly enough, the shaligram stones are considered a favourite of Lord Vishnu and an embodiment of his form. Vishnu, who was tied a rakhi by Adi Shakti, in her human incarnation as Devi Parvati, maintains a close connection to the Divine Goddess in this manner.

The Gandaki Devi Shakti Peetha at Muktinath is in an ancient temple that is built in the style of a pagoda, particular to the Himalayan region. The Muktinath temple is dedicated to Lord Vishnu and situated at a high altitude of 3,800 metres. It is one of the eight most sacred temples dedicated to Lord Vishnu, the other seven being Srirangam, Srimushnam, Tirupati, Namisharanya, Todatri, Pushkar and Badrinath. The tall idol of Vishnu here is made of gold and in the courtyard is a pond where the water flows in from the 108 faces of the bull, said to be depictions of 108 Shri Vaishnav temples. The temple is sanctified by the flow of River Gandaki which is a blessing of Devi Adi Shakti, and close to this Peetha, along with the Shri Vishnu temple, there also flow 108 sacred springs.

This magnificent pilgrimage site is a must-stop for visitors from all over the world and not confined to devotees of the Divine Goddess. It is equally venerated by Buddhists who know it by the name of Chumig Gyatsa which means something along the lines of 'a palace of water'. It is believed that the benevolent Gandaki Devi will fulfil any desire of those who pray to her with a true heart of devotion. All unfulfilled prayers will be granted and no visitor will return empty-handed. Adi Shakti here is the mother, the graceful, the grantor of all knowledge, for Gandaki Devi is the embodiment of all Siddhis or spiritual accomplishments. It is perhaps for this reason that this shrine is believed to be the place where one comes to attain great spiritual knowledge hoping that the Divine Mother graces the seeker with the path to enlightenment.

Muktinath resonates with a heavenly serenity surrounded as it is with snow-capped mountains. This is where the legend says that Maharishi Valmiki sat and penned the great epic Ramayana. It is also where the Ashvamedha horse was tied and allowed to rest. As the story goes, Maharaja Dashratha, the father of Lord Rama and an incarnate of Vishnu, wished to hold an Ashvamedha Yagna, which was the grandest of Vedic religious rites performed by a king, as a way of maintaining his supremacy among all kingdoms. According to the rite, an especially fine stallion was allowed to run wild across the boundaries of all kingdoms of a region, followed closely by the royal guard of the Maharaja. If any foreign kingdom dared to stop his great run, they had to either fight or submit to the Maharaja. When the horse from Ayodhya entered the kingdom of Mithila, which was ruled by Raja Janaka, the father of Devi Sita and incarnate of Mahalakshmi, he was extremely fatigued and at the brink of exhaustion. She encountered the horse and the great compassion in her heart stopped the Ashvamedha. It seemed as though the two kingdoms would be on the brink of war not ideal for a small peaceful nation such as Mithila, but through her own wisdom and wit, Devi Sita diffused the tense predicament and stopped the practice of the Ashvamedha Yagna. The Ashvamedha was tied in Mithila, given food and water to drink and Devi Sita herself tended to its wounds.

Gandaki Temple, Muktinath, Nepal
Photo: Creative Commons/Sagunkaranjit

Another story comes from *Devi Bhagvatam* about Tulsi Devi who fell in love with Lord Vishnu in his Krishna form and was later married to the Lord. Since then, she has always been worshipped alongside Vishnu in his Shaligram form. The Muktinath temple thus also finds mention in *Vishnu Purana*. It is said that the Shaligram stone which is needed to build the idol of Vishnu is formed here in the river by the downward flow of the currents in River Gandaki, which seem to be unique to this area.

The spiritual charge of the Gandaki Devi Shakti Peetha is steeped in the history of the Hindu faith, especially in the context of the Devi, for it is here in its lap that Devi Sita came to live in exile from Ayodhya, it is here where she gave birth to Luv and Kush, and it is here where they, the sons of Rama and Sita, gained divine knowledge from Maharishi Valmiki. In the festival of Navratri in the Chitra Mas (March–April) and the Ashvija Mas (September–October), devotees, especially women, come from all over Nepal, fasting in fervour in honour of the Goddess. The Devi's idol is decked in colours of orange, red and yellow, wreathed in garlands of flowers and jewels, with her eyes wide and tongue stretched out. She bestows all boons on those who come to her and offers them salvation from obstacles.

9

Jashoreshwari Devi Shakti Peetha
Jessore, Bangladesh

Om Maha Kalyai
Ca Vidmahe Smasana Vasinyai
Ca Dhimahi Tanno Kali Prachodayat

[Om Great Goddess Kali, the one and only one, who resides in the ocean of life and in the cremation grounds that dissolve the world, we focus our energies on you, may you grant us boons and blessings.]

—KALI GAYATRI MANTRA

Part of pre-partition Bengal, certain areas of Bangladesh have a deep devotion to the Great Goddess. A small town complete with its bustling street markets, narrow winding streets, road-side stalls of street food and kirana shops, Jessore—or as it is colloquially known, Joshor—is the quintessential picture of Bangla life. Jessore is not the sort of town that can be mistaken for a tourist favourite; it is however a transit point between Khulna and the Indian border at Benapole. The town itself offers a quaint geography to explore and a fine sampling of its local proletariat culture. Most visitors who come to Jessore enjoy the many archaeological sites here, including the remnants of Chanchara Rajbari, the Kali Mandir and the Dargah of Ghazi Kalu. Among the more interesting relics within the region are the remnants of King Mukut Roy's palace, dating back to the 12th century and Nawab Mir Julma's residence which, in comparison, is slightly younger, having been built around the 17th century. While each of these sights provide an experience of the many faiths, rulers and communities which had their impact on the culture of Bangla, many visit this part of the country for the Jashoreshwari Devi Shakti Peetha. It is in the village of Ishwaripur in Shyamnagar of Satkhira and is believed to be the Peetha which is believed to be where the left palm of the Devi lies.

The Jashoreshwari temple is an ancient site built in the 15th century under the patronage of the ruler of Jessore, Maharaja Pratapaditya. If legends are to be believed, then it is said that one day when Maharaja Pratapaditya was out surveying his kingdom, as was the practice among the royal heads at that time to understand the problems, trials and tribulations of their people, he discovered a luminous ray of light emanating from a woodland bush. When the Maharaja went to discover the source of the light, he found a piece of stone carved in the form of a human palm. The Maharaja's advisors told him to create a shrine for the engraved stone since it had to be the Devi's blessing for him to find. Maharaja Pratapaditya, who was a worshipper of Goddess Kali, built the Jashoreshwari Devi temple. Ever since, Jashoreshwari Kali has been known as the Goddess of Jessore and the town was named after her.

An ode to the Mahakali form of the Divine Goddess or Shakti, the temple was built by the Brahmin architect Anari. He built a 100-door temple for the Jashoreshwari Shakti Peetha. In time, it was modified by both Laxman Sen and Pratapaditya. In the late 13th century, Laxman Sen made a few changes to the structure. After the war and civil unrest in the year 1971, large parts of the temple crumbled. Now when one visits the

Jashoreshwari Temple, Bangladesh
Photo: Creative Commons/N Islam Photography

Jashoreshwari Peetha, the most prominent structures of its architecture are the pillars. A notable part of the remaining structure is the large rectangular, covered platform which forms the Natmandir, and has been erected adjacent to the main temple where the shrine rests. It is from this point that the face of the Goddess can be seen.

The Jashoreshwari Peetha has been described as the Goddess lotus-like hand; the Bhairava protecting her is Chanda. Since this is the spot where the Devi's hand is placed, it is believed to be a place of immense spiritual power for it is with her hand that the Goddess bestows her gifts. It is through the Abhaya mudra of her hand that she removes all fears and darkness. There is regular puja held on Saturdays and Tuesdays in the temple, which is usually done in the midst of a local gathering of devotees from the nearby villages and towns.

Jashoreshwari Shakti Peetha is open to all, despite the many sectarian divisions in the faith. Each year the temple is visited by thousands of pilgrims who congregate from all around Bangladesh and beyond, from the Indian subcontinent. The temple has an annual Kali Puja which is celebrated with much pomp and reverence. The Kali Mata worshipped at the temple is known to absolve the ego of her devotees, rid them of their sins and the maya or illusion of their existence, and grant them the ultimate goal of salvation or enlightenment. The form of Kali worshipped here is unique; her fierce form, her fire, is directed inwards, burning through the ego and the impurities of the mind. It is the Peetha that's representative of the spiritual journey of the atman to the parmatman. Jashoreshwari Devi, who is the 'all bearing', the 'all producing', provides us with the unshakeable foundation upon which to build our enlightenment. The Kali Puja is held in the months of Navratri in the Ashwija Mas, or the month of October.

There is also a rather popular mela or fair that is held annually in the temple complex in celebration of the benevolence of the Goddess. Families, pilgrims, and tourists alike gather from everywhere, dressed in their finest to celebrate the Goddess, to bring to her feet their sincerest prayers and to, as is hoped, return with her blessing and guidance.

10

Jayanti Devi Shakti Peetha
Jaintia Hills, Meghalaya

Anguli-Vrndam Hastasya Prayaage Lalitaa Bhavah |
Jayantyaam Vaama-Jangghaa Ca Jayantii Kramadiishvarah ||

[The anguli vrinda (group of fingers) of my hand fell at Prayaga. There the Devi is known as Lalitha, the one who is playful, and the Bhairava is called Bhavah, the essence of existence. At Jayanti, my vama jangha, or the left thigh, fell. There the Devi is known as Jayanti, or the one who is victorious, and the Bhairava is called Kramadeeshwara, or the lord who makes the world move forward.]

—PEETHA NIRNAYA TANTRA

Part of the Seven Sisters in Northeast India, the Jaintia Hills of the state of Meghalaya stand lush green on the boundary of its neighbour Assam in the north and east, Bangladesh in the south, and the East Khasi Hills on the west. This piece of hilly land—rich in minerals and vegetation—grows with the overwhelming fervour of the wild nature spirit that is felt on the banks the Myntang. Within the Jaintia Hills District is the village of Nartiang which used to be the summer capital of the Jaintia king, a place of respite from Jaintiapur, the actual capital.

Nartiang is most well known today as the summer getaway of the royal family. What was once a resplendent abode fit for aristocracy, stands in its mere remnants located on a hillock 2 km away from the Nartiang market. There are few details of the original architecture which tell us enough about the socio-cultural development of the region under the Jaintia kings. The archway of the summer palace makes use of the red bricks which were used by the Ahom kings of Assam. If legend is to be believed then it is said that the temple was built by the Jaintia king on his conversion to Hinduism. The framework of the temple was typical to the Khasi houses of the period, with a dieng blai, or central wooden pillar, and a thatched roof. In later times the thatched roof was switched up for a corrugated tin roof, which was further modified to resemble the steeple of a church.

The temple rises from a mound between old rocks and the dense green of the forest, and the waters of Myntang encircle it. It is believed that the river is the 'guardian angel' of the temple. She is the nourisher, the one bringing the forest in the surrounding area alive. There is a tunnel within the temple complex which leads on to the banks of the river. In ancient times, the temple had a long-standing tradition of human sacrifice, part of certain traditions of the Devi's worship. As prayers and incantation was offered to the Goddess along with a sacrifice, the blood would pool and flow into the waters of the river. Year after year, the blood would mingle with the vegetation of the mountainside, staining the sparkling water of the Myntang. It wasn't till British rule that human sacrifices as part of the worship of the Devi were banned. While the tradition continues to this day, it is now goats and other animals that are presented at the altar.

The temple itself is a simple structure, a red and white painted building that resembles a house more than the grandeur of a Shakti Peetha. Nonetheless, its reputation as an enormous silent power within the hills is widely acknowledged by the people living in the village and in the areas surrounding it. The temple dome is covered by a gold-plated sheath, perhaps the only hint of excess in the entire construction. The inner complex opens into a large courtyard and there are three caves in the temple. The first cave is dedicated to the tri-murti—Brahma, Vishnu and Maheshwar. The second cave is dedicated to Lord Shiva as Purush, and the third cave to Mahakali or Adi Shakti as Prakriti. The Devi here is worshipped as Jaintia Devi, deriving her name from the rulers of the region. She is a version of the fierce aspect of Adi Shakti, which is Mahakali. A Goddess of destruction or ultimate liberation, she demands immense sacrifice; hence the tradition of human sacrifice and now animal sacrifice which is part of the rituals and worship of this Peetha. As Jayanti Devi, she is the victorious and her Bhairava, Kramaadishwar, is the one who propels the world forward. For her devotees, the Devi clears the path to enlightenment, to being one with the divine spirit. Jaintia Devi is also know as Falizur Kalibari by the people of Meghalaya.

The rituals of the temple are not the same as the rituals performed for the Devi in the plains; rather they are an amalgam of Hindu and Khasi traditions. The local chief, or the syiem, is the principle patron of the temple. During Durga Puja, in honour of centuries-old tradition, the chief sacrifices goats in honour of the Goddess. This is the alternate form that was adopted by the priests when human sacrifice was banned. The human head used to roll to the goddess's feet in the inner sanctum of the shrine; today it is the goat's or duck's head that falls at the Goddess's feet. Interestingly enough, the goats are made to wear a human mask prior to being offered as sacrifice, harking back to a rather darker tone of the form of worship at the temple. During the festivities of Durga Puja, a banana plant is dressed up as the Goddess and worshipped in her stead. When the four-day festivities draw to a close, the plant is ceremoniously immersed in Myntang. At this time, a gun salute is given to the Goddess in an odd mix of traditional and modern.

The Central Puja Committee, which is the official representative of the Hindu community in Meghalaya, is responsible for looking after the temple. They manage the finances, upkeep and development activities of the temple and the temple complex. The Devi temple has become a popular destination in Nartiang and is visited by many. During the Durga Puja festivities it is decked in heaps of marigold.

II

Jwalaji Shakti Peetha
Kangra, Himachal Pradesh

Jvaalaamukhyaam Tathaa Jihvaa Deva Unmatta-Bhairavah |
Ambikaa Siddhidaa Naamnii Stanam Jaalandhare Mama ||

[At Jwalamukhi, in like manner, my jihvaa (tongue) fell. The Deva there is known as Unmatta Bhairava, meaning the Bhairava who is furious with intoxication or passion. The Ambika or Mother Goddess there is known by the name Siddhidaa, translated to the Giver of Siddhis. My sthana, or breast, fell at Jalandhara.]

—PURANIC TEXTS

Yet another powerful seat of the Goddess is in the Kangra valley of Himachal Pradesh. The temple is dedicated to the 'Flaming Goddess' form of the Devi or the Mother Goddess. As the giver of all Siddhis, it is in this form that she burns the egos of her devotees. As per legend, this was the place where Devi Sati's tongue fell after her self-sacrifice. Ever since, the Goddess occupied the place in the manifestation of nine flames. The Bhairava protecting her shrine here is Unmatta Bhairava and he is the intoxicated, the passionate, who in this form represents those who come to the Devi to be released from their maya or illusion.

The Jwalaji temple is built in the Indo-Sikh style of architecture on a wooden platform that resembles a pedestal. The structural design of the temple is pedantic, clean and minimal; perhaps this is one of the reasons that devotees experience such a strong and radiating aura of the Goddess. Despite the simplicity of the temple there are traces of the precious and divine in its build; for instance the dome and the spire are covered in gold. It is a belief among the people of Himachal that from the moment one gets closer and closer to the Jwalaji Mandir and can see her golden spire, their pilgrimage to her begins. Following this tradition, one can hear the chants and the songs of the Devi all the way to her ascension. At the entrance to the temple stand guard two stone sculptures of the lions that are the vahans or the vehicles of the Divine Goddess. Once inside the complex, in sparse touches of grandeur, the visitor is presented with the large main door to the shrine plated in silver, with carvings of episodes from the Goddess's life. Just before the shrine, there is a huge brass bell that was presented to the Jwalaji temple by the King of Nepal.

Nepal has long had close ties with the sect of Shaktism and more specifically the worship of Devi. The kuldevi or dynasty goddess for the Shahs of Nepal was a form of Devi very close to the Jwalaji temple. Socioculturally too, Nepal follows the tradition of Kumari, the living child goddesses of Nepal, which while a Buddhist tradition, is rooted in the Devi tradition. It is the Devi's maiden form that is worshipped, which is believed to pave the path for the communion with the divine.

Within the sanctified shrine of the Jwalaji Shakti Peetha, there lies a pit of burning flames; the offerings that are made to the Goddess are made in this pit. Many have tried to solve the mystery of the effervescent flames that are consistently burning, but nothing substantial was made of it. After much exploration it is believed that the flames are burning due to the release of natural jets of combustible gas, said to be prevalent in such mountainous areas. However such an occurrence has not been noted anywhere near the region, historically. Unique to this temple is the fact that there is no idol of the Goddess to pray to; rather she is considered to be residing within the flames of the pit. The temple priest lights the natural gas that comes from the mouth of a copper pipe and it is this flame that is worshipped as Devi Jwalaji. What is truly amazing about this Peetha is the eternal blue flame burning on the rocky side of the pit in what seems to be without any assistance. The interior of the shrine that holds a 3 ft-deep pit is surrounded by a pathway, its centre a hallowed rock, the main source from where the flames emanate. This is considered as the mouth of Goddess Mahakali. The subsequent nine flames never cease to burn, each named after a form of the Goddess—Mahakali, Annapurna, Chandi, Hinglaj, Vindhya Vasini, Mahalakshmi, Saraswati, Ambika and Anji Devi.

According to local legends, Raja Bhumi Chand Katoch, the ruler of the kingdom of Kangra was a great devotee of Maa Durga. Once in a dream he saw the sacred pit of Devi Jwalaji. Immediately on waking, he sent his men in search of this place. The spot they discovered was where the Raja built his temple to the Goddess. The temple was completed in the 19th century. It is believed that Maharaja Ranjit Singh visited it in 1809 and on this visit, he had contributed gold and silver for the dome, spire and the main doors. The temple itself was looked after by the princely state of Nadaun, Kangra. Once the independence of India was declared and the princely states dissolved, the site was deemed as a significant place of cultural heritage and the temple affairs were placed under the privy of the state government. A total of 102 priests have been appointed by the government for the management of the temple and its affairs.

There is a havan conducted in the temple daily and the Goddess is offered rabri or thickened milk, mishri or sweet candy, and seasonal fruits, as part of her bhog. The puja or the aarti is conducted in phases through the day; the first aarti or the Mangal aarti is performed at 5 a.m. in the morning, the next aarti or the Panjupchaar pagan is at sunrise, Bhog ki aarti where the Goddess is offered fruits, milk and mishri is at 7 in the evening, and the final aarti or Shaiyan ki Aarti when the Goddess retires for the evening is at 10 p.m. It is Shaiyan ki Aarti which is truly a beautiful affair, for one gets to experience the Devi's bed as it is decorated with beautiful ornaments and dressed for her rest. The first part of the aarti is conducted in the main shrine and the second part in the sejabhavan where she rests. Sankaracharya's great hymn—*the Soundaraya Lahri*—is recited along with portions of *Durga Saptashithi*.

An important pilgrimage for Hindus, devotees come in large numbers to pay their respects at Devi Jwalaji. In the days of Navratri, the temple is packed with crowds from all over the country. Colourful and rich fairs are organized in March, April, September and October.

12

Kalmadhav Devi Shakti Peetha
Amarkantak, Madhya Pradesh

Kaan cii-Desho Ca Kangkaalo
Bhairavo Ruru-Naamakah |
Devataa Devagarbha-[A]akhyaa
Nitambah Kaalamaadhave ||

[At Kanchi, my kankaala (skeleton) fell. There the Bhairava has the name Ruru. The Devata here, implying the Devi, is named as Devagarbha. The literal meaning of her name is the womb of divinity. At Kalamadhava, my nitamba (buttocks) fell.]

Amarkantak in Madhya Pradesh has an unusual landscape. It rests gracefully within the Vindhyas and the Satpura range of mountains, finally meeting at the edge of Maikal Hills. It is from this point where the rivers Son, Johila and Narmada emerge. In the illustrious history of this town are strong ties to the Bhakti movement in India. The great Bhakti poet of the 15th century, Kabir, was said to have meditated in the caves of the hilly terrain of Amarkantak at the Kabir Chabutra which literally translates as the platform of Kabir. It is a short distance from Chitrakoot, the town whose legacy stretches all the way back to the Ramayana, as the place where Lord Rama, Devi Sita and the devoted Lakshman spent 11 years and six months of their 14-year-long banishment period. Like Chitrakoot, Amarkantak, with its many ranges and hidden abodes within these ranges, was a popular sanctuary for sadhus, ascetics and yogis to come and meditate within. The lush green belt of flora and fauna in the town is known for its medicinal properties and is currently part of the Achanakmar-Amarkantak Biosphere Reserve.

It is believed that at Amarkantak, the left buttock of the Great Goddess fell. She is worshipped here in her ugr, or fierce, form. The Bhairava who protects the Devi is called Ashitanda. In the form of Kali, the Goddess is the embodiment of time and is known to devour everything. Interestingly enough, she is irresistibly attractive to not just the gods but also humans, which is perhaps why even in this form she is still the benevolent mother, protecting her devotees, her children, from destructive forces. She is represented as a three-eyed goddess, dark skinned, a fearful figure ready for battle, her neck adorned by a necklace made of heads, a skirt made of arms, her tongue lolling out bright red, holding up her scimitar and sword. She is the one who has defeated death, the gatekeeper of esoteric knowledge of destruction, creation and birth. Her devotees who come to her do so in search of salvation and release, for safe passage through the duality of the world.

The temple itself is almost as picturesque as the living environs in which it is situated. Like many Shakti Peethas, its external architecture is simple—clean lines and brick walls all painted in white; within the temple complex are ponds or kunds, and just outside is the bank of the river Son. There is a short climb of a hundred or so steps that brings one to the temple complex and the inner sanctum, greeted by a pillared entryway into the hallowed interiors of the Devi's chambers or the garbhagriha. The Devi is worshipped in her statuesque form made of dark stone, which is decked in bright red clothing. She is adorned by garlands of flowers brought by devotees from far and wide.

The Kalmadhav Devi temple is believed to date as far back as 6,000 years ago when it was built by a Suryavanshi king of Bundelkhand called Samrat Mandhata. However its history can be traced back to the fateful Prajapati Daksha's yagna. It is a melange of Devi worship and festivals such as Makar Sakranti, Sharad Purnima, Deepawali, Somvati Amavasya, Ram Navami and Navratri are celebrated with much fervour here. What is unique to this Shakti Peetha is the co-mingling of religious traditions stemming from both the Puranic times and the Ramayana, with a strong tradition which unites the worship of Devi Sita and Devi Kali. It is notable that Devi Sita herself was a great devotee of Devi Parvati, the benevolent form of Kali, and it is Parvati who she turned to when praying for a union with Lord Rama.

The Navratri festival falls twice a year, once in March or April, and the other time in September or October depending on the lunar calendar. This is a major celebration in Amarkantak which carries on for the entire nine-day period, with many devotees visiting the temple seeking the Goddess' blessing. For many devotees, the rituals and fasting are so severe that they refrain from eating any type of food that is derived from the soil. This is perhaps because Devi Sita, who is also associated with the worship here, was born from the Earth, or Bhumi-ja. At the end of this period of nine days, special ceremonies are conducted and rituals carried out. It is also a popular time for naming ceremonies for newborn children. As an offering to the Goddess, fruits, milk and homemade sweets are given, which are then consumed in the form of prasada. Another festival which is celebrated with equal gusto is Shivratri or the eternal night of the Shiva-Shakti union. During these auspicious days, many devotees throng to the temple while observing a nirjala vrat, or without drinking a drop of water. Lord Shiva and the Devi are worshipped together, bathed in milk, water, honey, ghee and curd, and offered the bilva leaf beloved to Lord Shiva and the

Dhatura flower that is presented only in his worship. It is believed that those who come to seek the blessings of the Goddess do not return barren.

13

Kamakhya Devi Shakti Peetha
Kamgiri, Assam

Yoni-Piittham Kaamagirau Kaamaakhyaa Tatra Devataa |
Yatraaste Tri-Gunna-Atiitaa Rakta-Paassaanna-Ruupinnii ||

[At Kamagiri is the seat of my yoni (generative organ).
The Devata (implying Devi) there is known as Kamakhya
(literally meaning the desire of creation). Here,
the Devi who is beyond the Three Gunas has taken the form of
Rakta Paashaan (Red Stone).]

One of the most powerful of Shakti Peethas, and also a site of tantric worship, the vagina of Sati fell here. Surrounded by the temples of the Dus Mahavidyas, Kamakhya has a number of myths and legends associated with the Great Goddess.

According to religious literature, the Kamakhya temple was built by Kamadeva, the god of desire, who was eviscerated by the opening of Lord Shiva's third eye, when he tried to help Devi Parvati win the favour of the Great Lord of Destruction. In his attempt to redeem himself with the help of Vishwakarma, the principal architect of the universe, Kamadeva built this temple in the Devi's honour and it was here that he once again regained his beauty and splendour. The original temple, as the legend goes, had a gigantic structure, much bigger than its present complex. It was an architectural wonder of sculptural magnificence. For a period which coincided with the rise of Shaivism among the rulers and the kingdom of Pragjyotisha, the Kamakhya Devi temple was said to have lost its significance. However its roots date back to the pre-Aryan times. Kamakhya Shakti Peeth, being the hallowed spot where Devi Sati's yoni fell, is a fertile ground for the worship of creation. Kamakhya Devyalaya or the temple is intertwined with some of the oldest oral histories and legends, its rituals and traits mentioned in ancient literatures such as the *Devi Bhagawatam, Devi Purana, Kalika Purana, Yogini Tantra* and *Hevajra Tantra*, to mention a few. Each source reflects the temple's importance in different eras and periods, and through different dynasties.

Historically, Kamakhya Shakti Peetha and the temple built around it seemed to have gained prominence in the times of King Naraka, the earliest paramount of the Brahmaputra Valley. While there are few evidentiary writings or oral records to support this patronage, there is a legend in *Kalika Purana* which relates to King Naraka whose father was Lord Vishnu and mother was Dharitri. After spending his childhood in Mithila, Naraka was believed to have come to Pragjyotisha at the behest of his father. Here Naraka defeated the Kiratas, who were believed to be the earliest devotees of Goddess Kamakhya and were led by their King Ghatak. Though King Naraka was a follower of Goddess Kamakhya initially, under the influence of Banasura, king of Sonitpur, he later began to grow egotistical about his power. The power corrupted him from within so much that Naraka was said to have prevented sage Vasistha from having darshan of the deity, because of which Vasistha cursed both the Goddess and Naraka. When the atrocities committed by Naraka became too much to bear, Lord Vishnu had to intervene and restore balance by killing his own son and destroying part of the temple. It is perhaps for this reason that there are few writings which delve into the patronage of the Naraka kingdom over Kamakhya Devi and it is only with the rise of the Koch kingdom in the mid-16th century that we get the early written and authentic records of the worship in the temple. Other historians believed that it was sometime in 500 CE that the temple was built in the Nilachal Hills, and it was perhaps due to natural calamities that the upper structure was destroyed, leaving the lower portion to gradually get buried under its own weight. Nonetheless, there is no doubt that the sanctity of Kamakhya Devi is renowned among Hindus and thousands and thousands devotees come to this ground each year in search of a union with the Goddess.

In a legend from *Yogini Purana*, Lord Brahma created the whole world, but soon he became proud. He started to believe that he was the supreme creative force of the universe. His ego was becoming the very force of his destruction and Jagatmata Mahakali created a demon called Kesi to bring back the balance. As soon as Kesi was created, he chased after Lord Brahma, threatening to swallow him up. In fear, Brahma Dev turned to Lord Vishnu to help him, just as the demon Kesi built Kes Puri, a demonic city torturing the world. Vishnu, realizing Lord Brahma's folly, advised him to pray to Devi Mahakali, to appeal to her for his redemption. Brahma, having come to the realization of his mistake, prayed to Mahakali, who appeared before him. Having destroyed the ego of the Dev, she now turned her attention to the insatiable demon Kesi, eviscerating him by Hum Kara. From the ashes, Brahma Dev built a hill green with grass, symbolizing his sin of the ego, which was now reduced in proportion. The Devi created a yoni circle out of her own creative force and told him to worship it, but blinded by his tainted ego, Brahma was unable to see the yoni. Through years of penance and tapasya, a luminous light finally revealed the yoni, which thereafter was worshipped by all as the divine creative force of the Devi as Kamakhya Mahakali. This place of worship was called Nilakuta Parvat or Nilachal, home to the Kamakhya Shakti Peetha.

Kamakhya Temple
Photo: Creative Commons/Kunal Dalui

Kamakhya Devi is also a seat of tantric worship. The Devi is popularly known as the goddess of desire or one who grants all desires. As such, she is also worshipped as Maa Tripura Sundari and called Shodashi. In the middle chamber of the temple, which is also known as the Pancharatna, is an image of the Goddess who is depicted in her youth, 16 years old with 12 arms and six heads, five of which look ahead and the sixth atop the rest. She sits on a lotus which is emerging from the corpse of her consort Lord Shiva. Shiva's body itself is lying on top of a lion, the vahan of the Goddess. The Devi is dressed in a red sari decorated with red hibiscus flowers, and she holds a lotus, trident, sword, bell, discus, bow, arrows, club, goad and a shield in each of her ten hands. She also has a bowl made of gold from which she bestows her goodwill, and a skull which symbolizes her victory over death.

In the garbhagriha or the hallowed centre of the temple is the fissure of a rock which symbolises the yoni of the goddess, the actual form worshipped here. A small spring runs beneath it, washing the rock with water. The yoni is placed facing north even though the temple faces eastward, and the rock is kept covered by a sari decorated with flowers and sindoor, or vermilion. The Goddess is worshipped according to both Vamachar and Dakshinahar i.e. the left hand path or tantric, and the right hand path or the usual form of worship. Part of the worship in the Kamakhya Devi temple includes the sacrifice of buffaloes, goats, monkeys, tortoises or pigeons—all male, since female sacrifice is unacceptable here, and preferably black. This is perhaps because Kamakhya is a form of Mahakali, the fierce goddess of war and vengeance. It is part of the daily offerings to her. Unique to this Shakti Peetha is a truly terrifying practice which was common in the days of the yore, one of ritual human sacrifice, where men were sacrificed to satiate the hunger of Kamakhya Devi.

There are three main festivals celebrated here; most important among them is the Ambuvachi or Ambubasi or

Ameti, which is the three-day period beginning from Saptami in the month of Ashadha of the Hindu calendar, roughly around the end of June in the Gregorian Calendar, when the Goddess undergoes her menstrual period. The water of the natural spring turns red and the yoni is covered with a cloth. The temple remains closed for those days. It is considered inauspicious to till the ground or plant seeds during this time, but on the fourth day, a great celebration is held. The sindoor or vermilion and pieces of the cloth that covered the Devi's yoni are given out as prasada, considered as a blessing from the Goddess. This period is also considered extremely significant in tantric practices. The second significant festival is Navratri, when women from all over India congregate at the Devi's temple, worshipping her many forms, dressed in their finest, offering bangles, bindis, sindoor and other such forms of shringara, to the Goddess. Finally comes Dev Dhvani or Debaddhani, the festival conducted for Manasa Devi, in the months of Jyeshtha, Asadha, Shravana and Bhadrapada, also considered a time of pestilence and disease by farmers. The festival received its name from the tremendous sound created by the sound of instruments such as the drum and the dhol during its celebration, when the Goddess is appealed to look after the harvest. Worship of the Goddess at any time of the year is believed to bring the fulfilment of all wishes, but the Kamakhya Devi is specifically known to bestow fertility and prosperity on her female devotees who tie bronze bells on the trees within the temple complex. The best time to visit Kamakhya Shakti Peetha is from November to March, when the weather is temperate and the festivities at an all-time high.

14

Kankalitala Devi Shakti Peetha
Bolpur, West Bengal

Om Maha Kalyai
Ca Vidmahe Smasana Vasinyai
Ca Dhimahi Tanno Kali Prachodayat

[Om Great Goddess Kali, the one and only one, who resides in the ocean of life and in the cremation grounds that dissolve the world. We focus our energies on you, may you grant us boons and blessings.]

—KALI GAYATRI MANTRA

The temple town of Kankalitala is located a short distance of 8 km from Shantiniketan in Bolpur, West Bengal. As a settlement town built on the banks of River Kopai on the Bolpur-Labpur road, this is where another one of the Devi's Shakti Peetha is enshrined. As per the legend of the Daksha yagna, after the self-immolation of Sati when Lord Vishnu released the Devi's body from the desperate grasp of a grieving Lord Shiva via his Sudarshan Chakra, it was on the hallowed grounds of Kankalitala that Devi's waist bones fell, creating in its wake a town known among the Shaktas, the sadhus and the yogis for its piety and devotion.

Colloquially the town is known by the name of 'Kankali'; 'kankal' in Bengali means skeleton. It is considered that perhaps the town was named after the presence of the Shakti Peetha of the Devi and as such is believed by the devotees to exist under her protection and benevolence. Listening to the legends and lores pertaining to the Kankalitala Devi Peetha, it is believed that the waist bone of the Devi fell to the ground with such great force that it created a depression in the Earth from which a lake sprung forth, known here as a kund. It is in the depths of this kund that the Devi's Peetha actually exists. However, for the purpose of worship, just opposite the lake, a temple was built in honour of Devi Parvati. Many devotees believe that the bones of the Devi can still be found at the bottom of the pond, although no one can confirm it. Though the date of origin of this temple has not been formally recorded, it has remained a place of worship since anyone can recall.

Interestingly, there have been attempts towards the destruction of this Shakti Peetha in a manner similar to the destruction that was faced by the Kamakhya Devi temple. According to Mughal records, Kala Pahar, the ferocious general of the Delhi Sultanate army known for destroying Hindu temples as a symbol of the establishment, had, alongside the Kamakhya temple, destroyed the upward base of the Shiva lingam of this temple. This happened in the 16th century when Bengal was under the rule of the Afghan Pathan warlord, Sulaiman Khan Karani, under the reign of the Mughal Emperor Akbar. Kala Pahar, born as Rajiblochan Roy, was a conflicted personality who, when he converted to Islam and adopted his new identity, went on to, as part of his conquest runs, destroy temples and symbols of devotion such as Jagannath Puri, Kamakhya and Kankalitala.

The Kankalitala Shakti Peetha is perhaps the simplest of all the 51 Shakti Peethas, with its unadorned edifice rising up in a pyramidical construction, sparsely ornamented by a metallic spire. The garbhagriha or the inner sanctum—its literal translation meaning a womb chamber—is a small room. Connected to it is the Natmandir which serves as an area for devotees to stand in and receive the darshan of the Devi. On any given day, one finds this area to be the busiest in the temple with visiting devotees and sadhus napping in its shade from the punishing heat of the sun. This is also the area in the temple where many yogis and sadhus sit in deep meditation or sadhna, being in such close contact with the Divine Mother.

On entering the garbhagriha, one is faced not with a three-dimensional figure of worship in the form of a sculpture or a stone, metal, or clay depiction of the Goddess, but a framed image of the Devi in her Mahakali form, standing atop the form of her husband Lord Shiva. Whilst the image that the pilgrims pray to is of Mahakali, it is her benevolent and domestic form of Maa Parvati who is truly worshipped here. She is accompanied by her husband Lord Shiva or Shambhunath, who is represented as the Bhairava Ruru. When wondering about the dissonance between the two forms of Kali and Parvati, where one can be considered a fearsome force of destruction and the other a gentle force of creation, we are only to understand what the priests of the temple believe—which is that both these forms represent one being, and that is the Devi. The great Divine Goddess is in all her forms a mother, a creator, a force of destruction, a force of seduction, and so much more. She is the Mahadevi and the embodiment of everything.

The lingam of Bhairava Ruru used to be magnificent in size, however after the encounter with Kala Pahar, it is a relic of survival, deeply entrenched into the ground. The devotees pour water and their offerings on the pit of the broken lingam. A place of immense calm and tranquility, its marble floorings are often used as a rest stop by travelling pilgrims, who come to this Shakti Peetha as part of the pilgrim circuit of the Shaktas in West Bengal. Much in the tradition of the past, even though it is a place of worship of Devi Parvati, there is within the sanctity of the temple the Harikath or the place where the animal sacrifice is offered to the Goddess. This has become less frequent now. There are also various ceremonies of death that are carried out here, since the temple does have within its complex a fully functional crematorium.

What is notable about this particular Shakti Peetha is the fact that even though the icon of devotion of Kali or Parvati is placed within the garbhagriha of the temple, the most sacred object of worship here lies in the kund built within the temple complex. The kund does not run very deep and is protected by a concrete wall topped with a red fence to prevent people from jumping in.

Kankalitala is a place of worship of the Devi, which has a truly democratic nature, in that it is beloved to both the householder and the tantric, the wedded bride and the sadhu, the kanya and the widow. People from different walks of life, stratas of society, privilege and devotion come to the Devi's abode.

15

Kanyashram Shakti Peetha
Kanyakumari, Tamil Nadu

Kanyaashrame Ca Prsttham Me Nimisso Bhairavas-Tathaa |
Sarvaannii Devataa Tatra Kurukssetre Ca Gulphatah || ||

[At Kanyashrama, my pristha, meaning back, fell, and the Bhairava there is called Nimisha, meaning a moment of time. The Devata, here implied as the Devi, is known as Sarvani, meaning the wife of Shiva.]

In the southern tip of India, on top of a hill surrounded by the sea, is the temple of Devi Kanyashram—Kalikashram, or the Kanyakumari Shakti Peetha. The Devi is worshipped here as Sarvani, the literal meaning of the name being the wife of Shiva. Her Bhairava is Nimisha. This was the place where it is believed that the Devi's back fell, and while the island itself has changed over time, the original architecture and structure of the temple remain intact. The temple is dedicated to a form of the Devi which is closer to the form of Durga among her many forms. Not too far off from this is another Shakti Peetha of equal splendour called Suchindram. The art and architecture of Suchindram, like that of the Kanyashram, stands apart, in that it is unique and blends elements of Tamil culture within it in terms of the sculptures depicting the gods, their dance-like forms, the mudras, etc., chiselled in stone with finesse. The red dome-like structure of Kanyakumari stands against the waves which wash up to its shore, creating a peaceful melody which adds to the tranquility of the Devi's temple. Such is the religious significance of this temple that each year, millions of people flock to its shore to pay their respects to the great Divine Mother, the Goddess Sarvani.

According to the legends of the temple, when Banasura, the king of demons, had managed to obtain a boon from Lord Shiva by which he could only be vanquished by a virgin, he went to inflict sufferance on the people on Prithvi. Unable to witness the asuras tormenting the villagers, Goddess Parashakti took the form of a virgin girl and came to the shores to perform a penance. Lord Shiva took the form of Suchindrum, who was to marry the Goddess, and the wedding was accordingly fixed at an auspicious hour before dawn. Devarishi Narada, realising that the wedding would foil the purpose of the Devi's incarnation, heralded the break of dawn before the actual hour, which spoiled the muhurat of the wedding, therefore postponing it. Lord Shiva returned and the Devi resumed her penance by the rocks on the shore, which are now called Sripadaparai. Banasur, meanwhile, had heard about the beauty of the girl in penance and came to ask for her hand in marriage, but the Devi rejected her suitor. The demon king decided to win her by force. It was this attempt that led to a fierce battle between the Goddess and the demon, in which the Goddess prevailed. Sripadaparai is now known as the Swami Vivekananda Rock, and it is at this spot commemorating the Devi, that her holy feet are enshrined. People who come to worship her here are known to take a dip in the ghat which marks the confluence of the three seas, the Arabian Sea, the Bay of Bengal and the Indian Ocean.

The structure of the temple, set by the edge of the ocean, is rectangular and walled on the sides. About 3,000 years ago, the original temple structure was destroyed by the constant erosion caused by the waves of the ocean beating against the temple and the effect of the strong gusts of sea winds corroding the stony structure. There is a small pyramidal gopuram which rises above the main temple pointing the way towards the inner sanctum of Kanyashram. The deity is placed facing eastwards as per the scriptures. One enters the complex from the northern gate of the temple; the eastern gate of the complex remains closed all year round except on certain occasions which are usually festive and when the deity is taken out for her ceremonial bath. This is the gate used exclusively for the Devi. Additionally, the reason why the eastern gate remains closed all year round is because in the past, many ships have been wrecked here, because they mistook the brilliance of the temple's nosing for a lighthouse.

Kanyashram is one among the tourist circuit of South India as mentioned before. The Suchindram temple dedicated to Lord Shiva is a short 12 km away from the temple. There is a Ganesha temple that is located within the complex of Kanyashram. As Sarvani Devi is the benevolent aspect of Durga, closer in form to Parvati, her familial ties of mother are represented through the presence of Lord Ganesha close at hand. There is also a small pond of sweet water located on the seashore in the temple complex, called Pushkarni or Manduk Tirtha Sthal. It is considered sacred by many. It is believed that these waters perform various miracles, such as healing ailments, in fertility, sinus, etc.

There are some specific rituals which are particular to Kanyashram. Due to its unique location as a point where the three seas meet, devotees visiting Kanyashram bathe in the ghats which hold the waters from the three seas. There are 25 teerthams on the shores leading to Kanyashram. Teerthams are the sacred representations of the deity; in this case, of the Devi. These come in many forms. In Hinduism, it is believed that the divine exists in every organism and is the microcosm of

Kanyashram Kanyakumari Temple
Photo: Creative Commons/Coolgama

the world. The teerthams of Kanyashram are made of stones. The rituals and systems are in accordance with the Namboothiri priesthood of Kerala, which are derived from Vedic scripts and belief systems.

Navratri is celebrated with much aplomb for a period of nine days marked by festivities, lights, music and women decked in fineries coming to the shores of Kanyashram. This usually happens in the Ashwija Masa, that is in the months of September–October. Special pujas and yagnas are conducted during Durga Puja and Vijayadashmi. Kanyashram also has a particular festival dedicated to the celebration of cars and transport vehicles called Kala Bham festival held in the month of Aadi which is from mid-July to mid-August.

16

Kiriteshwari Devi Shakti Peetha
Murshidabad, West Bengal

Utkale Naabhi-Deshan-Ca Virajaakssetram-Ucyate |
Vimalaa Saa Mahaa-Devii Jagannaathas-Tu Bhairavah ||13||

[At Utkala, the portion of my nabhi (navel) fell, and the place is known as Viraja Kshetra. The Mahadevi (Great Goddess) there is known as Vimala (literally meaning stainless, spotless, pure), and the Bhairava there is Sangbarta (the one who brings the end of the world)[3].]

The Kiriteshwari temple is among the oldest and holiest temples to visit in the district of Murshidabad, West Bengal. The state of West Bengal has an enormous culture of Devi worship and some of the most significant Shakti Peethas. This temple is located in Kiritkona village near Lalbagh court road in Murshidabad. What is interesting about the Shakti Peetha is that it is known as an Udapeetha, which is a Peetha where no anatomical part of the Devi fell, but rather an ornamental part. The temple is an auspicious spot, representative of the Devi and thus a metaphysical space of worship. It is one among a handful

---

[3] https://greenmesg.org/stotras/durga/shakti_peethas.php

of temples in West Bengal where no actual deity is worshipped; rather it is an auspicious stone that is the representative form of the Devi and the object of worship.

According to the mythology of the place, it was here that the crown or the kirit of Sati fell. The Devi is worshipped here as Vimala or the pure, untainted one. The Bhairava is Sangbarta or Sambarta, the one who brings the end of the world. There are many popular names used for Kiriteshwari temple such as Mukteshwari temple and Kireetkana. In a piece of medieval literature, *Vabisyapuran*, the temple is mentioned as a place blessed by the Devi herself. From the recorded accounts, the construction of the temple is nearly a 1,000 years old. The place is said to be where the Mahamaya or the grand illusion of Shakti was resting or asleep. Many of the locals believe that when the Mahamaya awakens, she will rise from this temple. They also associate her with Mahisasura Mardini, the fierce form of the Devi.

The Maa Kiriteshwari temple was built in the 19th century by King Darpanarayan Roy. It was later renovated by the King of Lagola, Yogendranarayan Roy, and thrived under his patronage. According to local accounts, the old structure of the temple was destroyed in the year 1405. Devi Kiriteshwari is the Kuldevi or presiding deity of the ruling house of Murshidabad. Devi worship was at the height of its glory when they presided over the district. Devotees came from far and wide in hundreds and thousands to pay their respects before the great Mother Goddess. It is a tradition which, to this day, has thrived. Adjacent to the Kiriteshwari Devi is the temple of her Bhairava, which is small and modest and not kept up as well as the Devi's temple. It is situated on the shores of River Bhagirathi.

According to Puranic tales told and re-told in Murshidabad, during the wedding ceremony of Lord Narayana and Devi Lakshmi, the sages Lomas and Subrita were also invited to join the auspicious celebrations. They both arrived at the same moment and the host attended to Rishi Lomas before attending to Rishi Subrita. This enraged the latter and he developed eight crippled parts in his body. Henceforth he was known as Ashtabakra or the eight-curved Muni. Rishi Subrita roamed the Earth till he reached Kashi to meditate upon Lord Shiva. When the sage arrived in Kashi though, he was directed by a divine omnipotent voice to proceed to Gupta Kashi, which was eastwards. This brought him to Bakreshwar in Bengal, where he meditated for 1,000 years. Pleased by his penance, Lord Shiva gave darshan to the sage and granted him relief. Many believe that the divine voice was of Devi Kiriteshwari.

The popular festivals held at the temple include Durga Puja, Amavasya Puja and Kali Puja. On the day of the Amavasya, a special ritual is held dedicated to the Devi as the start of a new cycle with the new moon. The Goddess is offered anna bhog and an all-night yagna vigil is held. Apart from this, since the time of Raja Darpanarayan, the Kiriteshwari fair has been held every Tuesday and Saturday in the month of Poush, in December or January. This fair is held on the banks of River Bhagirathi and has been held since the time of Raja Darpanarayan. It is also a popular attraction for tourists who bathe in the waters of the river offering prayers and also join in the festivities.

The Goddess is worshipped in the form of a stone covered by a veil, which is changed only on Ashtami of each Durga Puja, after the Devi is given her sacred bath. There is a high altar on which we find a small altar. This is where the form of the Devi resides, and where the kirit as the object of worship is placed. Interestingly enough, the crown of the Devi, the kirit, has been worshipped through the ages. It has always been worshipped in the same form. One notable caretaker of the headdress was the zamindar-philanthropist Rani Bhabani, who preserved it in the Guptamath opposite the temple. Rani Bhabani was known for her generosity and is believed to have constructed hundreds of temples and resthouses across Bengal. She was generous in her contribution to water tanks and educational institutions, and had a role to play in the upkeep of Kiriteshwari temple too, though there are few accurate records of her involvement.

17

Kottari Devi Shakti Peetha
Hinglaj, Pakistan

Brahmarandhram Hinggulaayaam Bhairavo Bhiimalocanah |
Kottari Saa Mahaa-Deva Trigunnaa Yaa Digambarii ||

[My Brahmarandhra, that is the aperture on the crown of the head, fell at Hingula, where the Bhairava is called Bhimlochana, literally meaning the one with fearful eyes. There the Devi is known as Kottari. She is the Great God, the embodiment of the Three Gunas, she is Digambari, the one who directs us beyond.]

—PEETHA NIRNAYA TANTRA

Kottari Devi is the goddess who accepts all in her embrace, from different communities, sects and religions, in modern-day Pakistan. Lyari Tehsil is the remote hilly area of Pakistan's Baluchistan province, about 250 km northwest of Karachi, 19 km inland from the Arabian Sea, and 130 km west of the mouth of the Indus. It is within the narrow gorges of Lyari's rocky terrain that the ancient temple dedicated to Kottari Devi, the Hinglaj Mata temple, is located. The temple is situated under the protected jurisdiction of the Hingol National Park at the end of the Keerthar Hills by River Hingol.

Before the independence of India, the Partition struggle and the subsequent formation of Pakistan in the year 1947, the region which constitutes modern-day Pakistan had a large Hindu and Sikh population inhabiting it. After Partition, this number fell to about 3 million because of the migration of nearly 6 million Hindus and Sikhs to the newly formed India. Of these, nearly 2.3 million were Hindus, largely concentrated in the district of Tharparkar (Thar) within Sindh province. It is these people who form the largest contingent of pilgrims visiting Kottari Devi annually. While Kottari Devi is worshipped by all from different classes, communities and walks of life, many of the visiting pilgrims to this temple are bonded labourers and farm workers. The attire of these people living in the rural settlements of Pakistan, in what is a treacherous and punishing mountainous desert landscape, is strikingly colourful and bright. The women are dressed in their finest heavily embroidered clothes with bangles stacked on their arms as they come to pay their respects to Kottari Devi. For the Thari children, many of whom are employed as bonded labour from a young age, this is a once-in-a-year fun expedition and a time to see the world beyond what they know.

The pilgrim's journey to Hinglaj Mata temple serves as a purpose of bringing people from all walks of life together; it is a meeting point for doing community work in the name of the Goddess. The opening up of a large-scale community kitchen for the purpose of seva or the practice of selfless service, brings together pilgrims. Each year, hundreds of volunteers come together for this devotional purpose. In the kitchens, vast quantities of food such wheat rotis, rice dishes, sattvic vegetables and lentil soups are cooked for thousands of pilgrims each day. Historically, few could make the gruelling journey across the Makran desert to Hinglaj, where part of Devi Sati's head is believed to have fallen. When they finally arrive at the destination, it is as though they have arrived within an oasis of faith, a sanctuary and a place of rest from the troubles of the world. In recent years, notably the infrastructure of the province, the roads and the connectivity have improved by leaps and bounds and the journey to Hinglaj has become less taxing and more comfortable.

Uniquely enough, Kottari Devi at the Hinglaj temple belongs not only to the Hindus and Sikhs of the region, but is equally popular among the local Muslims living in the area, who both revere and protect Hinglaj Mata. The locals know her as Bibi Nani (maternal grandmother), and the temple is considered as the Nani temple. Bibi Nani may very well be the Goddess Nana, who appeared on Kushan coins and was widely worshipped across both West and Central Asia. The local Muslims, in fact, join in on the pilgrimage and call it the 'Nani ki Haj'.

There are many legends and stories that surround the Hinglaj Mata temple. One among them explains how the place received its name. The story talks about two princes, Hingol and Sundar, who were from the Tatar Mongol clan, living sometime in the Treta Yuga. They spent their days tormenting people due to their thirst for strife. To free the people from the tyrants, Lord Ganesha, the Devi's younger son, killed Sundar, whose death drove Hingol mad with a thirst for vengeance. The terror among the people grew even greater and in their desperation they appealed to the Devi, the Great Goddess and Divine Mother, to put an end to their suffering. The Devi, unable to see her devotees in pain, descended on to the battlefield. After warring with Hingol, she lured and trapped him in a cave, where she brought an end to his unrelenting ego and his life. In his last moments, with the clarity of one whose ego has been completely destroyed, Prince Hingol prayed to the Devi, requesting her to name the cave—the place which was bound to become a sanctified place of her worship—after him, so that he may always be associated with her. Since then the cave where the idol of Kottari Devi is worshipped is called Hinglaj Devi temple.

Another legend of the Hinglaj temple testifies to its ancient

Kottari Devi (Hinglaj Mata) Temple, Pakistan
Photo: Creative Commons/Abrar Alam Khan

roots in the Dwapara Yuga. It is said that when Parashuram was on his killing spree, bringing an end to all kshatriyas who were maddened and corrupted by power, Ratnasena, the king of Sindh, arrived at the ashram of Rishi Dadhichi with his children, seeking shelter. Mistakenly, Ratnasena, in this time of exile, stepped outside the premises of the ashram and was instantly killed; his sons though remained safe within the boundaries. On entering Rishi Dadhichi's ashram in search of King Ratnasena's sons, Parashuram found that there were only Brahmins in the asharam; the kshatriya sons were given protection in the guise of Brahmins by Hinglaj Mata and from then on, were known as Brahmakshatriyas or warrior-priests. One of the sons of Ratnasena, Jayasena, returned to Sindh eventually to rule the kingdom, armed with a protective Hinglaj Mata mantra given to him by Rishi Dadhichi.

Kottari Devi as Hinglaj Mata is a protective and benevolent deity who bestows goodwill and protection upon her devotees. While Hinglaj is her most prominent temple, in the neighbouring Indian states of Gujarat and Rajasthan, she is worshipped in shrines as Hingula, Hingalaja and Hingulata, and as the Red Goddess Kottari or Kotavi. The Kularnava Tantra which mentions the 18 Peethas of the Devi, mentions Hinglaj as the third one, where her Bhairava, Bhimalochana or the one with fearful eyes, protects and venerates her.

Inside the sanctum of the Hinglaj cave, the Devi's idol is not one that is man-made, rather it is a small shapeless stone worshipped as Kottari Devi. The stone is smeared with sindoor or vermilion. Pilgrims who come to worship come bearing traditional red banners of the Devi, wearing the distinctive red and gold scarves covering their heads. With the newly built Makran Coastal highway, what was once a long and treacherous journey was made a mere four-hour drive from Karachi. Every year 25,000 to 30,000 pilgrims come to the temple to pay their respects, some come in private cars and buses, a few on two-wheelers and cycles, and the most austere of devotees make the journey on foot, all to be graced by the deity, the Divine Mother, who is known to end the ego and bless those who come to her with enlightenment.

18

Mahamaya Shakti Peetha
Amarnath, Jammu and Kashmir

*Kaashmiire Kannttha-Deshan ca
Trisandhyeshvara-Bhairavah |
Mahaamaayaa Bhagavatii
Gunna-Atiitaa Vara-Pradaa ||*

[The above quotation signals the entry into a deeply spiritual space of Mahamaya—which is illusion. It says at Kashmir, my kanthadesha (region of the neck) fell. The Bhairava there is known as Trisandhyeshwar. The literal translation of his name is the Lord of the Three Divisions of the day: dawn, noon and sunset. The Goddess who resides there is known as Mahamaya or the Great Enchantress, and she is beyond the three gunas—Sattva, Rajas and Tamas—the giver of all boons.]

—TANTRA CHUDAMANI

As I travel through the sacred geography of India, the 'Mother', 'Maa' and 'Devi Maa' dot the landscape and I seem to be instinctively drawn to the mythology of the shrine. Within Indic tradition, the narrative of the story adds a deeper emotional connect to the more intense experience of the divine feminine force.

The Devi Peetha located in the holy cave of Amarnath in Jammu and Kashmir is one of the most significant Shakti Peethas. This is the holy spot where Devi Sati's kanth or throat fell. Sati, who is worshipped here as the Mahamaya or Great Illusion, is the all-perfect Goddess who can both create and destroy maya or illusion, offering devotees the path to enlightenment, beside her Lord Shiva, who is worshipped as Trisandhyeshwar.

The Amarnath Shakti Peetha is situated at an altitude of 12,756 feet and about 140 km from Srinagar. There are two routes to reach Amarnath cave—one goes through Baltal, a mere 70 km from Srinagar, and the second route goes through Pahalgam, Chandanwari, Sheshnag and Panchatarani, and is a journey of 94 km by bus. The route between these two, going through Pahalgam, is relatively easier compared to going through Baltal. From Chandanwari, located at an altitude of 9,500 feet, another 16 km has to be travelled by foot to reach the cave temple. Every year, the state government organizes an annual Amarnath Yatra to facilitate thousands of pilgrims who arrive from all over the country to have a darshan of the ice lingam. The cave is open for darshan during the month of Ashada to Shravan Poornima (July–August) for a period of 45 days which is considered the most auspicious time.

The Amarnath Cave is one of the most venerated shrines in India dedicated to Lord Shiva and the Devi, with many mentions through the ages. The cave itself is surrounded by a landscape of snowy mountains. Inside the cave is the ice stalagmite, a type of rock formation that grows vertically from the floor due to the freezing of water drops falling from the roof of the cave to the floor. The Amarnath Cave is about 15 feet in height and 60 feet in length and breadth and in the shape of a rectangle. The ice stalagmite, which is the Shiva lingam, swells and increases in size from the month of May to August and decreases thereafter. It is said that the size of the lingam in the cave changes depending upon the phases of the Moon and is at its maximum height during the hottest months of summer, its expansion and contraction changing with the seasons.

At the northern tip of India is the Peetha of Mahamaya located at the staggering heights of the Amarnath Cave. There are many local legends and lores surrounding the rather mystical environs of the cave. According to one such legend, Devi Parvati wanted to know why her beloved Shiva wore the Mund Mala, the garland around his neck made of heads. Shiva replied that each time Parvati had taken birth, another head was added to his mala. Devi Parvati was astonished on hearing this and asked Lord Shiva how was it that she was experiencing this continuous cycle of life and death while he was immortal, and pleaded with him to share this eternal mystery of life and death. Lord Shiva, rarely able to refuse Parvati anything, was willing to share this most sacred knowledge with her as long as it was in a place where no living being could hear it, and thus he chose the icy sanctuary of the Amarnath Cave. As Lord Shiva and Devi Parvati began their journey towards the Amarnath Cave, he started to release the many symbols which adorned him one by one. First he left his vahan or the vehicle he rode, Nandi the bull, at Pahalgam, which is also known as Bailgaon. At Chandanwari, he released the crescent moon from his great jata or dreadlocked hair. He released his snake on the banks of Lake Sheshnag and left his son Ganesha at Mahagunas Parvat, widely known Mahaganesh Hill. Finally, at Panchtarni, Lord Shiva released the panchbhoota or five elements—earth, water, air, fire and sky—which make up both the Earth and humans. It is believed that Shiva and Parvati did the Tandava Nritya as a symbol of sacrificing the panchbhootas. The Tandava Nritya is the cosmic dance, the source of the cycle of creation, preservation and dissolution; in performing it, Shiva and Parvati relinquished the elements.

Shiva and Parvati were now ready to enter the deep Amarnath Cave. In the cave, Shiva took samadhi on his deerskin mat. He wanted to keep the immortal tale a rahasya or secret, so he created the Rudra named Kalagni, ordering him to spread a fire that would eliminate every living thing present around the holy cave. Only when he was satisfied that only Parvati and he himself were present, did he begin to unravel the mystery of life and death. Unbeknownst to him however, there was an egg lying beneath the deerskin, which had escaped the ravages of Kalagni's purifying fire. It was considered non-living, and the protection offered to it by Shiva and Parvati's own asana ensured its life. The pair of pigeons born out of this egg became immortal after having heard the secret of immortality, or the Amar Katha, from Lord Shiva. To this day, many devotees who visit Amarnath report having sighted the pair of pigeons enroute to the ice lingam.

A more popular story is that of the union of Devi Parvati and Lord Shiva at Amarnath. Lord Shiva was leading an ascetic's life after the death of Sati, when she was reborn as Parvati, the daughter of Himavan. She had to undertake severe tapas to reunite with Shiva. After 16 years of austerity at the Amarnath Cave, Shiva finally appeared to her and accepted her as his wife. It was here that she became Mahamaya, the Great Enchantress. Another local tale goes of a shepherd by the name of Buta Malik, who discovered the Amarnath Cave in the 15th century. A saint gave Buta Malik a bag full of coal, which later turned out to be a bag full of gold once the shepherd reached his home. On seeing this transformation, the shepherd ran back towards where he had met the saint to thank him, but by then the saint had disappeared, leaving no trace of his presence. In his place, Buta Malik found the holy cave of Amarnath and a Shiva lingam. Thereon, all the villagers in the nearby villages worshipped the transforming lingam. It is colloquially believed that the saint was the great Lord Shiva himself.

In *Rajatarangani*, a historical chronicle written in verse form in Sanskrit by the poet Kalhana, which talks about the kings of Kashmir and their reign, one describes Amarnath as a significant place in the lives of the people. Kalhana mentions King Samdhimat Aryaraj (34 BCE–17 CE) who used to worship a lingam made of ice 'in the region above the forests'. This lingam of ice is referred to as Amareshwar or Amarnath in other places. Further in the text, Kalhana tells us of Queen Suryamathi, the wife of King Ananta (1028–1063 BCE), 'granted under her husband's name agraharas at Amareshwara, and arranged for the consecration of trishulas, banalingas and other [sacred emblems]'.

Around Amarnath and the Mahamaya Shakti Peetha are various other holy sites in an intimate conclave for pilgrims, such as the Martand temple dedicated to the Sun God; Chandanwari, the place where the rivers Sheshnag and Asthan converge; the Sheshnag Lake itself, along with Pishu Ghati. These are places of victories in faith where the danavas were defeated by the devas. Among the important festivals celebrated at the Mahamaya Peetha is the festival of Nag Panchami. After the Chhari Puja, which is the worship of Lord Shiva's silver mace, pilgrims move into the final stage of the journey to Amarnath. The story of the Chhari, like most legends connected with the Mahamaya Shakti Peetha and the Amarnath Shiva lingam, is one that is both divine and human. Once while descending from his Himalayan abode, Lord Shiva met a lame man who would not move out of his way fast enough. In a flippant retort, Lord Shiva commented on the man's hesitant movements. With deep humility, the man said that if he had a silver walking stick like the Lord, he would too move with great speed. Lord Shiva thought this through and with even greater humility than the man, handed over his silver mace to him. It is believed to have been passed down from generation to generation, revered as the symbol of the

God to whom everyone is equal, as well as a symbol of the Amarnath Yatra, bound to make the journey up and down for as long as it is meant to be.

19

Phullara Devi Shakti Peetha
Attahas, West Bengal

Attahaase Ca-Ossttha-Paato Devii Saa Phullaraa Smrtaa |
Vishvesho Bhairavas-Tatra Sarva-Abhiisstta-Pradaayakah ||

[At Attahasa, my ostha (lips) fell. The Devi there is remembered as Phullara, which literally means blooming like the flowers. The Bhairava there is called Vishvesh, which literally means the Lord of the World. The Devi who resides there is the bestower of all wishes.]

—PEETHA NIRNAYA TANTRA

'Attahas' is a Sanskrit term which is derived from the words 'Atta' and 'Hasa' or laughter, especially implying loud laughter. According to legend, Devi Sati's lower lip fell here. Since then it has become a temple of significance as a Shakti Peetha, and in West Bengal it is part of the pilgrimage circuit for all those who are devoted to the Devi, or as she is known in these Peethas, as Adi Shakti. The Shakti of this shrine is also known as 'Phullara' for she blooms like the flowers, bestowing her bounty on her devotees. The Kaalbhairava guarding this Peetha is called 'Vishvesh,' or the Lord of the Universe.

Phullara Attahas is about 150 km from Kolkata, and is a great draw for tourists. Located in close proximity to the Devi temple is the Vishvesh temple, protecting the Peetha for all eternity. The Phullara Peetha is remote enough to mimic a journey into the inner depths of one's internal universe. It is connected to the world only by road; the closest railway station is in the Ahmedpur district. Hopping onto a bus at the Nirol bus station, which is the nearest, a mere 5 km from the temple, devotees come in hoards to visit Mata Adi Shakti, the great Divine Mother. There are limited routes that one can take to Phullara Peetha. From the railway station at Ahmedpur, the only way forward is through local transport. Many devotees flying in via the Netaji Subhas Chandra Airport, which is about 160 km away from Labhpur, are forced to change their mode of transportation in order to reach the Peetha.

The Attahas Peetha is unique due to the serenity and union with nature that surrounds it. The temple itself is amidst the wild woodlands and vegetation of West Bengal, just off the banks of River Ishani. The forest beside the temple premises is known to be rich in diversity with various species of birds and plants to be found, to the extent that many believe it to be blessed and protected by the benevolence of the Goddess herself.

In this Peetha there is no consecrated form of the Devi; she is embodied in stone, which is of a magnificent build and size, symbolic of the lower lip itself which about is 15–18 feet wide. Maa Phullara is the one who is blooming. She is symbolic of life and revival, of growth and transcendence. Her Bhairava and consort, Lord Vishvesh Mahadev, is shown seated on a lotus in a temple adjacent to the shrine. The temple is sans grandeur: one does not find any architectural marvels or aesthetic display of stone work here, and yet the tranquility of its surrounding has a way of enveloping even the most burdened of its visitors.

As the story of this Shakti Peetha from the Krittibas Ramayana goes, in the Treta Yuga when Rama was at a stand-off in battle with Ravana, he wanted to have the blessings and assistance of Devi Durga in her fierce form as Chandika. Despite his deep earnest prayers, the Devi would not be appeased; she refused to appear before Shri Rama. It was then that the learned and devout Vibhishan counselled Rama that he worship the warrior form of the Goddess with 108 blue lotuses. Lord Rama called on Hanuman to assist him in procuring these blue lotuses, for which Hanuman, it is believed, came to the Phullara Peetha, to the pond beside the temple, the only place where one could find blue lotuses, and brought 108 of them back for Lord Rama as per his request. Half-way through his puja, Lord Rama found that there were only 107 blue lotuses and he was one short. The human incarnate of Vishnu the preserver knew he had to undergo the tests of the Devi to prove not only his devotion to Adi Shakti but also his love for Sita. To complete his puja, Lord Rama began to carve out one of his own eyes which resembled the lotus to place at the Devi's altar. At this moment the Devi appeared and stopped him, granting him the boon that she would leave the side of Ravana, allowing him to defeat him and rescue Devi Sita.

While the Shakti Peetha is a site popular among Hindu pilgrims all year round, the month of December is particularly favoured by visitors. Magh Purnima is celebrated with much fanfare and festivities for a period of ten days; it is the night of a full moon in the Hindu month of Magh. In the Gregorian calendar, it falls sometime between the months of January and February. This is considered rather auspicious all around India, and it is within these days that every 12 years the grand celebration of the Kumbh Mela is undertaken. At the Attahas Phullara Shakti Peetha, a 10-day fair is organized annually around Magh Purnima, known as the Phullara Mela, which sees visitors assembling from far and wide, having travelled for days in hoards to be granted a glimpse of the Divine Goddess.

The Navratri celebrations are conducted with a deep spiritual love here. Devotees worship the Devi, the Adi Shakti, in all her nine forms with music, dance and stringent fasting as the ultimate expression of their bhakti. For many, this is the defining point in the Hindu Calendar and many special pujas and havanas are inducted at the Navratri fair at this Peetha. Many worship the Goddess by not consuming anything that is grown underground during the entire nine-day period of Navratri. For the prasada, the offerings made to the Devi are usually grown from the soil. What is particularly unique about this Shakti Peetha is that in addition to the traditional offerings made in the form of prasada to Phullara Devi, many devotees offer sour foods and delicacies to the Goddess, believed to be favoured by her.

20

Ratnavali Shakti Peetha

Hooghly, West Bengal

Om umamaheshvarabhyam namah, om gauraye namah

[Salutation to Uma, the wife of Maheshwar or Lord Shiva, salutations to Gauri, the benevolent Goddess.]

This is yet another Shakti Peetha in the land of Bengal. Along the riverbanks of the Hooghly, under the leafy shades of vegetation, are the cobbled marketplaces leading to a number of ghats and piers which get maddeningly crowded in the early hours of the morning and the twilight hour of the evenings. There, on the tempestuous waters of the river, one finds parked jetties which operate as tourist ferries, and just beside them right there on the waters of the ghat are people amidst their prayer and rituals, taking a dip in the water and preparing for the day. On the stairs by the river are groups of socializing devotees, locals playing cards and visitors conducting their last rites. Amidst this most palpable model of the transient nature of life and death is the Ratnavali Shakti Peetha.

According to the legend of the Devi, it was here in the sacred Hooghly district on the banks of the river Ratnakar that Devi Sati's right shoulder fell to the ground. The temple commemorating her is known locally as the Anandamayee temple. The name of the temple in itself means the Goddess who gifts pleasure or happiness, and is in Khanakul-Krishna Nagar. The Devi here is Kumari, the 16-year-old or pre-adolescent form of Devi Parvati. She is the embodiment of the divine consciousness that is spread all across the universe, the consciousness that creates the universe. As the story surrounding the temple of Kumari goes, the Goddess created the universe from her womb, as such she exists equally in animate and inanimate objects. The Goddess is said to reside in all female beings as creators, according to *Devi Mahatamya*, and often as part of her worship, especially during the Navratras, nine young, pre-adolescent girls are made part of the ritual. They are fed, prayed to and receive gifts. While *Devi Purana* declares all female beings as auspicious, it is usually the younger girls who are made part of the worship because they represent purity and chastity. Unmarried girls aged between one to 16 years, are said to be bereft of desire, worldly pleasures and anger; they highlight the importance of women.

It is also interesting to note that in the rituals to the Devi, while one mostly experiences the worship of an idol or an inanimate representation of the Goddess since we believe she exists in all things, it is in worshipping conscious beings as are represented by the human kumari that there is utmost sanctimony and which is closest to her personal worship. In many ways, the worship of the human forms of the Kumari Devi is the worship of the divinity of human potential, and of the heights that mankind can reach through spiritual efforts and honest steps towards attaining enlightenment.

As is the norm, every Shakti Peetha has a shrine dedicated to Bhairava in his different manifestations. Here the Bhairava is not just the Devi's consort but also her spiritual guru, for all depictions of the kumari in Puranic tales and legends show the Devi as a devout worshipper of Lord Shiva. As part of her worship, red sarees and oil wick lamps are offered to the Goddess, and verses from *Devi Bhagavat Purana* are recited while circumambulating the shrine.

21

Mahishamardini Shakti Peetha
Birbhum, West Bengal

Vakreshvare Manah-Paato Vakranaathas-Tu Bhairavah |
Nadii Paapa-Haraa Tatra Devii Mahissamardinii ||

[At Vakreshwara, my manas (mind) fell. The Bhairava there is called Vakranatha (literally meaning the Curved Lord). There, the river removes the sins, and the Devi is known as Mahishamardini (literally meaning the Destroyer of Mahishasura).]

The Bakreshwar, or the Mahishamardini Shakti Peetha, is located near Birbhum district in West Bengal, on the banks of the river Papahara (literally meaning 'remover of sins'). This Shakti Peetha enshrines the portion between Devi Sati's eyes, also known as the third eye, which fell in this particular spot when her body was incised into 51 parts by Lord Vishnu. There are varying beliefs as to which body part resides here, as some believe it was a part of the brain that actually came to land at Bakreshwar during the immolation. Here, Devi Sati manifests herself in the rupa of Mahishamardini. The Shakti Peetha is situated close to Bakreshwar temple, one of the most revered places of Shiva bhakti, where he is locally worshipped as Bakreshwar (literally meaning 'bent' or 'curved').

The legend of the temple follows the story of a crippled muni, who was called Ashtabakra, literally meaning eight curves. While wandering the Earth and in search of Gupta Kashi in the east, the muni came to Bakreshwar and immersed himself in deep meditation upon Shiva for close to 1,000 years. Shiva was highly impressed by the sage's devotion and proclaimed that before worshipping Shiva, all devotees who visit Bakreshwar should worship Ashtabakra, in order to receive his blessings. This is perhaps the reason behind the presence of two lingams within the sanctum—the larger one known as the Ashtabakra lingam, while the smaller one is called the Bakreshwar lingam.

Bakreshwar in West Bengal is primarily known for the Shiva or Bakreshwar temple and the surrounding therapeutic geothermal springs, rather than the Mahishamardini Shakti Peetha. Even today, there are several residents of the state who visit Bakreshwar for Lord Shiva's darshan, and remain unaware of this very significant Shakti Peetha in the country. However, for those who are aware of the Shakti Peetha, the pilgrimage to Bakreshwar is particularly significant as it is a deeply spiritual site where the energies of the masculine and feminine divine, the traditions of Shiva and Shakti, unite. Another popular tourist attraction at Bakreshwar is the geothermal springs that surround the temple complex and are said to have healing properties.

Facing the Shiva temple is the Shwet Ganga Kund, which is perhaps the most frequented as it is used for purification baths by pilgrims due to its proximity to the temple. Next is the Dudh Kund, which is popularly known as the colour-changing kund as the water here acquires a pale white hue during dawn. The unique colour-changing quality of this kund is proof that the water has a high concentration of minerals, which can provide relief and healing to people suffering from various diseases and ailments. Another well-known kund in the area is the Agni, or Fire, Kund, where the water naturally boils at a high temperature of 200°

Fahrenheit. The kund is known particularly as a suicide site. The other kunds are Khar Kund, Bhoirob Kund, Shurjo Kund, Papohara Ganga and Jibhotsa Kund. The religious landscape of Bakreshwar attracts not only followers of Shaiva tradition, or worshippers of the feminine divine, but also suffering individuals who look towards the geothermal springs for relief.

Unlike most of the architecture in Bengal, the Bakreshwar and the Mahishamardini temple display a strong influence of Oriya temple architecture. The Bakreshwar temple features a white curvilinear tower with a shikhara, or a pointed spire, on the top. The garbhagriha, or the inner sanctum, is where the two lingams, Ashtabakra and Bakreshwar, are enshrined. The Ashtabakra lingam covers the smaller Bakreshwar lingam and they are both placed within a concave yoni in the centre of the room. It is believed that the Ashtabakra lingam made of stone is bent at eight different points along the length, similar to Ashtabakra Muni's body with eight bends.

The Mahishamardini temple has a similar curvilinear structure with a shikhara, but is distinct in its bright orange colour. The entrance of the temple is through the Bakreshwar temple, as well as through a separate entrance, which brings one directly to the orange and yellow gate of the temple. The temple has double wooden doors with six hand-carved friezes, featuring images of Lakshmi, Saraswati, Ganesha and Kartikeya. The garbhagriha of the temple houses the sacred murti of Mahishamardini, cast in a special alloy called ashtadhatu, which is an amalgamation of eight metals of astrological significance: gold, silver, copper, zinc, tin, iron, lead and mercury. The Goddess is depicted along with a lion, which was her vahan, and is shown slaying the buffalo demon, Mahisha. The 10-armed Devi is ferocious and powerful. While one hand holds the Mahisha-killing spear, the other nine have been left empty on purpose, as a way of allowing visitors to add miniature weapons as an offering during their darshan.

However, the presence of the Goddess is not only in the

murti, but also in the specific body part of Devi Sati—the portion between the eyebrows, that supposedly fell at this particular location. This Shakti Peetha lies concealed within the marble pedestal over which the murti has been placed. The pedestal features a small hole in which resides a smooth and round stone formation that juts upwards in the centre. The structure, which corresponds to the ornamented lunar crescent present between the deity's eyebrows, is in fact the adirupa, or original form of Mahishamardini.

In the same way, as with most Hindu gods and goddesses, the offerings are modest and simple: incense, flowers, sindoor, bangles, fruit and water. What, however, is unique to this particular goddess is that devotees are also allowed a unique and rather interactive offering, which requires one to place a tiny weapon of their personal choice in any of the nine remaining hands of the Devi. These weapons are available for purchase in the market near the temple.

22

Chamundeshwari Shakti Peetha

Mysuru, Karnataka

*Sarva Mangala Mangalye, Shive Sarvartha Sadhike,
Sharanye Tryambake Gauri
Narayani Namostute, Narayani Namostute,
Narayani Namostute*

[Oh Gauri Maa, consort of Lord Shiva; you who bestows auspiciousness in all, and fulfill everyone's wishes, I prostrate myself before thee, I salute you, take me under your care.[4]]

On the outskirts of Mysuru in the state of Karnataka are the scenic Chamundi Hills, an increasingly prominent place of worship and pilgrimage—the Chamundeshwari Shakti Peetha. The topography of Chamundi Hills draws as much from the Devi as the temple does from its hallowed location. The mountainous terrain resembles the form of the sleeping Devi, and the natural life that thrives in this hillscape has some of the most beautiful and rare herbs and flowers. It is this delicate ecosystem of Chamundi which requires one to ensure that there isn't rampant industry because of the draw of the spiritual tourism, for it is only too easy to trample the uniqueness of

---

[4]*Devi Mahatamya*, Sri Durga Saptasati-Chandi. Opening Sloka: 7

the place. The temple itself is a Krouncha Peetham, one among the Mahapeethas of the Devi, as collated by the mystic scholar-sage Adi Sankaracharya of the 9th century, in his great tome *Shakti Peetha Stotram*, one of the most well-known works on the non-dualism of Advaita Vedanta philosophy.

Goddess Chamunda received her name when she defeated the demons Chanda and Munda who were generals of the two mighty asuras, Shumbha and Nishumbha. The latter were vanquished by the Devi in her Durga aspect. Devi Chamunda is one of the Saptamatrikas, a group of seven Mother Goddesses who represent Shakti or the female counterparts of the male gods in Puranic texts, namely *Varahana Purana*. Chamunda is a warrior Goddess who is ruthless and bloodthirsty and usually associated with her consort, Yama, or the god of death. The worship or sect of the Saptamatrikas is most robust in southern India, in the regions of Tamil Nadu and Karnataka. The seven sister goddesses here have an independence from the male consorts and are worshipped by devotees for good health and progeny. This is a key distinction in their worship in South India versus their worship in North India where they are rarely seen in the absence of their consort or male counterparts. Chamundi Hills is where the locks from Devi Sati's hair fell from her charred corpse.

The Chamundeshwari temple was built and consecrated under the patronage of the royal family of Mysuru. An integral part of the Devi's worship is the practice of jatra or pilgrimage. In the 12th century under the reign of the Hoysala dynasty, which ruled from around 1006–1346 CE in the Southern Deccan region, the initial temple structure was built, and later in the 17th century it was further enhanced with notable structures such as the steps leading up the hill, which is extremely popular among tourists, especially those who love a good trek. Once again in the 19th century under the Wadiyar dynasty's rule, Krishnaraja III added the intricately carved entrance gopuram or tower. With

Chamundeshwari Temple
Photo: Creative Commons/Sanjay Acharya

its bright gold highlights, the temple can be spotted from a long distance. It shines forth like a beacon, inviting tourists, pilgrims and visitors into its powerful embrace. As a way of remembering his legacy, there is a rather life-like statue of the king which greets all visitors stepping upon Chamundi Hills.

Since Chamunda Devi is also looked upon as the chief mother of the seven mothers via the Saptamatrikas, she is also the kuladevi of the Wadiyar dynasty, flanked by Ganesha and Kartikeya, the two sons of Shiva and Parvati. There are many ritual traditions which were established by the family, such as the custom of drawing the sculpted lion chariot or simhavahana which was given to the temple sometime in the 1840s during the grand Dussehra celebrations in the city of Mysore. It was in the 17th century that Dussehra was first celebrated with such grandeur in Mysore. The Wadiyar king was inspired by the magnificence of religious celebrations in the neighbouring empire Vijayanagar.

Dussehra, which is also known in Hindu calendars as Vijayadashmi, marks the victory of Goddess Durga and is a concluding celebration of the nine-night festivities of the Navratras. In Mysore, beautifully decorated elephants and horses would be drawn through a procession. The royal weapons would be worshipped, and the Devi would be revered with grandiose festivities displaying the empire's wealth and military strength. As much as it was a time of spiritual oneness with Shakti, it was also a key political demonstration of power.

The Devi Chamundeshwari as the royal kuldevi was worshipped as much for her benevolence as her fearsome power. In fact, back in the days of the great empires, there was a thriving culture of animal sacrifices similar to that of the Vijayanagar empire. These traditions continue, except with certain modifications in step with contemporary times—now the king ritualistically sacrifices not an animal but a pumpkin to the the sacred fire of the havan, as he lays a branch of the Shammi tree at Chamundeshwari's feet instead of bones. Even today, the Maharaja of Mysore inaugurates the Navratra celebrations with a puja at Chamundeshwari Shakti Peetha.

There are many traditions surrounding the inauguration of the Navratra celebrations at Chamundi Hills, such as a wrestling match which is held before the celebrations. Some believe that it stands in for the banned custom of human sacrifice which is part of the cult of Chamundi. As the grand procession continues in all its finery through the town, Dussehra in Mysuru is a grand spectacle which draws tourists from all around the country.

As one draws closer to the temple, the gopuram shines forth brightly; the sculpted imagery of the Saptamatrikas, with Devi Chamundi on top, look out on the approaching visitors. The silver-plated gateway with the many faces of the Devi carved into the metal is guarded by the dwarapala, or the door-keeper, and Lord Ganesha. The inner sanctum of the temple is located within gold-plated brass doors. Here she is offered marigolds and coconuts by her devotees with the more affluent visitors even offering fine jewels, gold and silver.

The Devi, who is rarely seen in the absence of her consort Bhairava, is in close proximity of the Mahabaleshwar shrine, which houses a lingam and the Nataraja sculpture. The iconography of the Saptamatrikas surround the walls, with Parvati and Ganesha. The Mahabaleshwar temple is said to predate the Chamundeshwari temple, to a time when Chamundi Hills were called Mahabaladri, and the temple is attributed to the Ganga dynasty.

23

Katyayani Shakti Peetha
Vrindavan, Uttar Pradesh

Namah sivabhyam pasupalakbhyam
Jagatrayiraksanabaddhahrdbhyam
Samastadevasurapujitabhyam
Namo namah sankaraparvatibhyam

[At Vrindavan, my keshajaala, or tresses, fell, and there the Devata, here implying the Devi, is called Uma, whose name means 'with splendour and tranquility'. The Bhairava here is Bhutesha, whose name means the Lord of all Living Beings. The Devi there grants all Siddhis, or spiritual accomplishments.]

—UMAMAHESHWARA STOTRAM[5]

In the sacred geography of Hinduism, it is evident that most temples are either atop a mountain or on the banks of a river. The Katyayani Shakti Peetha is situated on a riverside. On the banks of the sacred Yamuna in the region of Braj, Uttar Pradesh, is the holy city of Vrindavan. Its deep-rooted ties to the Indian mythos have been explored extensively through Puranic kathas, for it was here that Sri Krishna was born. To

---

[5]https://stotranidhi.com/en/uma-maheshwara-stotram-in-english/

this day it is believed that his etheric body and spiritual energy have mingled with the air of the city, leaving its mark as a focus of faith. Along with its neighbouring city Mathura, Vrindavan has become a gathering place for pilgrims who come to visit the dozens of temples both old and modern which crowd its streets. As one of the most significant holy cities of India, it represents the plurality of Hinduism which is incomplete in the absence of a Devi sect. The white marble temple in the midst of the city is the Katyayani Peetha. The Goddess here is known as Uma, who is the benevolent form of Parvati, and the site draws its immense sacred energy from the locks of Devi Sati which are believed to have fallen here.

The Devi in her many forms as a consort to Shiva represents the many facets of Shakti: She is Uma, Durga, Parvati, Gauri, Kali and more. As a daughter of the Himalayas, she is Parvati or 'of the mountains'. It was believed that when Devi Parvati had made up her mind to earn the love of Lord Shiva, she went to the mountainous terrain of Himalayas to carry out the most stringent forms of sadhana to purify herself from the traps of the ego and the illusion of the world. Watching her beloved daughter who had grown up in the comforts of the palace, Menaka, the apsara wife of Himavan, cried after her daughter, 'Oh, Maa! Oh, Maa!' giving the Devi yet another identity.

The Devi is the primordial source of all creation, Adi Shakti; her power is her discernment for what must be sustained and what must draw to an end. She represents the cyclical nature of life and each form of hers is a facet of that cycle. On the slopes of Himavan's Himalayas, Shailputri transforms into Uma, who can also become Durga as she fights against Shumbha and Nishumbha—the fluidity of the forms is a representation of the fluidity of chita shakti, or the primordial shakti.

Mahishasuraa Mardini, who was called on jointly by all the devas of Indraloka, and the holy trinity—Brahma, Vishnu and Shiva—to slay the buffalo demon Mahishasura, was also Durga,

Mahadevi and Katyayani. The holy city of Vrindavan is a land which has a rich tapestry of its own myths and legends with towering figures such as Krishna and Radharani being part of the city's mythos. The tales of the worship of Devi as Katyayani are interwoven into the signature legends of Krishna and Radharani, for whom the pilgrims travel to the city all year round.

Before we begin to unravel the myth of the Katyayani Shakti Peetha, we have to delve into the legend of Krishna and Radharani. In the Puranic traditions, Sri Krishna was one of Lord Vishnu's ten avataras, and a guide to Arjuna on the battlefield of Mahabharata. Vrindavan was the city of his birth and its name literally means 'a grove of Tulsi trees,' beloved to Vishnu. Here, Krishna was raised by his foster parents Nanda Kishore and Yashoda, who were cowherds and raised Krishna as the apple of their eyes. In this idyllic village of Vrindavan, Krishna was meant to meet his divine and pre-ordained love, Radharani, one of the village girls who was an incarnation of Goddess Lakshmi.

Krishna was born in prison because his maternal uncle Kansa believed that the child born to his beloved sister, Devki, was meant to bring about his doom. He thus had her imprisoned in order to avoid such a fate. Devi Katyayani was instrumental in Krishna's fight against Kansa, which was representative of good versus evil, to restore harmony in the world. One key intervention of the Devi's maya was when Kansa, blinded by his fear, tried to end Krishna in his mother's womb. Lord Vishnu requested the Devi to take his place and with her eternal power, no harm could come to baby Krishna. This mingled her stories with that of the Krishna avatara and when it came to bringing about the end of Kansa, Sri Krishna sought the blessings of the Devi just before he killed his uncle.

The folklore of the Katyayani Peetha is rich and varied. It describes Radharani's worship of the Goddess. She had prayed to the Goddess to obtain the perfect partner for herself, who in her case was Krishna. Her tapas is what is today the viddhi of the sacred Katyayani Vrata, dedicated to the Goddess. Scores of devotees offer their prayers in this manner to the Devi so that they may too be reunited with their destined partner.

The Katyayani temple in Vrindavan was recently renovated since its consecration in February 1923 on the full moon day of the traditional lunar month of Magh. The site is expansive and spacious and has distinct pillars in black with rounded arches. The entrance is guarded by two golden lions, the Goddess' vahan or celestial vehicle.

The temple holds five idols within it, each a representation of a unique faction of the religious tradition in what is known as a Sampradaya in eastern philosophy. The main idol of Goddess Katyayani is made of ashtadhatu, or eight metals, and the Devi holds a chandrahas sword in her hand, a weapon with which, it is believed, she slices her devotees' egos. Beside her is the idol of her consort, Bhairava Bhutesha, and in the complex, there are also idols of Lord Vishnu, Lord Ganesha and the Vedic sun god, Surya.

24

Vishalakshi Shakti Peetha
Varanasi, Uttar Pradesh

*Vaaraannasyaam Vishaalaakssii Devataa Kaalabhairavah |
Mannikarnnii-[I]ti Vikhyaataa Kunddalam
Ca Mama Shruteh ||30||*[6]

[At Varanasi, the devata implying the Devi, is known as Vishalakshi, whose name literally means with large eyes, and the Bhairava is Kaalbhairava. There, where my kundala, or earring, fell is well-known as Manikarni.]

One of the most ancient cities in the world, Varanasi, Benaras, or Kashi, is also the city of moksha or final liberation. It is also the city of Shiva and Shakti.

Varanasi is a city of spectacles, culture, spirituality, and those seeking the spiritual within. It is on the holy banks of the river Ganga, on the ghats where one can observe the devout in their acts of worship and rituals. Just beyond the Meer Ghat, at what is known as Lahori Tola, is a temple shrine which is dedicated to the Devi in her Vishalakshi form. The Puranic kathas attached to this temple explain that this was where Devi Sati's karna kundala or earring fell, and the quantum

---

[6]https://greenmesg.org/stotras/durga/shakti_peethas.php

of power carried within the Devi's physical aspect turned this ground into one of her Shakti Peethas. However, there have been debates as to whether it was an ornament of the Devi or a part of her that actually fell on the grounds of this temple.

As in the case of all Shakti Peethas, the Devi's pind or body part, representing her essence, is protected or accompanied by her consort, Lord Shiva, who, in this Vishalakshi Peetha, is known as Kaalbhairava. In this depiction of Shiva, 'kaal' means time and Bhairava is the angry, destructive aspect of Shiva, a trait that is often associated with the god Yama, the deity who rules over the realm of death. Kaalbhairava's presence here is a reminder of the ultimate mortality of man, the transience of the lived experience and the fact that what has a beginning also has an end. Not too far away from the shrine is Manikarnika Ghat, named after the bejewelled earring of Devi Sati. It is a short walk from the Vishalakshi shrine and is a site which draws tourists, spiritual seekers and the devout all year round. Varanasi is one of the few cities in India so acclaimed for its place in the annals of Indian spiritual philosophy, that for many in the Indic tradition, it is a privilege to have their end met in Varanasi or the last cremation rites carried out in the city: this is believed to be a path to heaven. All day long, one sees funeral pyres burning on the ghats and beside the Vishalakshi temple, one finds those in mourning rubbing shoulders with those in celebration.

Returning to the disputed part of the Devi's pind associated with this temple, the name Vishalakshi roughly translates to 'the one with big eyes'. Now, it is believed that the Devi's eyes fell at the two Naina Devi shrines, one in Nainital in Uttarkhand and the other in Himachal Pradesh; however, many say that the third eye of Sati, the seat of spiritual sight, fell in Varanasi. It was on the spot where the third eye fell that the Vishalakshi shrine was built.

Goddess Vishalakshi is part of the three Mahadevis foremost in the Shakta tradition—Meenakshi, Kamakshi and Vishalakshi. Out of the three, Vishalakshi is lesser known and yet all three are worshipped using the same sacred geometric design which is a widely prevalent feature in the tantric tradition, known as the Sri Chakra Yantra. Devi Meenakshi who was an incarnation of Parvati and is also known as the 'fish-eyed goddess', was meant to marry her divine consort Shiva. It is this marriage which is depicted in the temple art that is found in the Vishalakshi Shakti Peetha, tying the two goddesses together.

The Vishalakshi Peetha is known for its rather distinct structure with a high-rising gopuram above the main worship sanctum. The renovation of the temple which was undertaken in the year 1970 was done so with the sponsorship from Tamilian community members of the Shakta sect. The sculpture of the Goddess is made of black stone and was established in the temple around the time these renovations were made. Right beside the black stone sculpture of the Devi is an older, more natural stone sculpture which was the original depiction of the Devi in her shrine. The eyes, one can observe on closer inspection, are defined via paint, having been coloured a prominent bright gold.

There is, within this temple complex, a sculpted form of Devi Lakshmi, consort to Lord Vishnu, in marble. During the festivities of the Goddess, when a procession is taken out through the city of Varanasi, a sculpture of Devi Vishalakshi is taken out in a horse-drawn chariot with much pomp and revelry. On the walls of the temple are a series of lingams, representing Shiva, and mantras depicting the sacred geometry of the Devi are etched into the temple pillars. Interestingly enough, within the structure of this shrine, one can also find drawings of celestial bodies associated with traditional lunar astrology prevalent in an earlier time in India. It is believed that to visit the Vishalakshi Shakti Peetha along with Kashi Vishwanath, Dandapani, Dundiraj and the Ganga is akin to performing Shashtang Yoga, a gesture of complete submission to the divine.

25

Kalighat Shakti Peetha
Kolkata, West Bengal

Kaaliighaatte Munndda-Paatah
Krodhiisho Bhairavas-Tathaa |
Devataa Jaya-Durga-[A]akhyaa
Naanaa-Bhoga-Pradaayinii

[At Kalighata, my munda (head) fell. There the Bhairava is called Krodhisha, which literally means the Lord who Possesses Anger. The Devata (implying Devi) is known as Jaya Durga, whose name literally means the Durga who is Victorious. She is the bestower of various worldly enjoyments.[7]]

In the great metropolis of Kolkata, the city brought to life by Shakta worship, stands the Kalighat temple. The beautiful house of worship is on the banks of a creek which was once part of the mighty Hooghly, before it changed its route many centuries ago. The creek is now called Adi Ganga, meaning the ancient Ganga. At this holy ghat in the southern part of Kolkata, it is believed that Devi Sati's mukha khanda or 'head' fell, which makes it an Adi Peetha—one among the four most significant sites of the Devi's worship. The Kalighat temple

---

[7]https://greenmesg.org/stotras/durga/shakti_peethas.php

Kalighat Temple
Photo: Creative Commons/Ankur P.

that we see today has been there since 1809; it was built on the hallowed ground of a 16th-century temple, a humble mud hut dedicated to the Devi. Here the Goddess is worshipped as Dakshina Kali, a form of the Devi particularly popular in this region of Bengal.

The image of Goddess Kali, especially as Dakshina Kali, has its roots in tantric worship as a fierce and frightening force of nature. She is the grotesque Mother Goddess, the primordial energy. Over time, she became one of the foremost deities revered in Puranic texts, fascinating poets, scholars, writers and priests alike for decades and centuries. In the 16th-century text, *Brihada Tantrasara*, by Krishnananda Agavamavagisa, we get a graphic depiction of Goddess Kali through the Kali Tantra. She is described as one with a garland of heads adorning her breasts as she holds a head in one hand and a sword in another. Devi Kali is the Samsana Kali, the naked, dark-skinned Goddess found on the cremation grounds, often seated on a corpse. As a nod to this aspect of the Devi, right beside Kalighat, one can find one of the biggest cremation grounds of Kolkata. She is Digambari, with her long billowing hair, crimson, warm, blood dripping from her fangs, a belt of severed arms wrapped around her waist. She is the form of the Mother Goddess who is the personification of death and destruction, evoking fear in the hearts of wrongdoers.

In Puranic texts, Devi Kali is associated with Lord Shiva's consort Devi Parvati. This association is delved into in *Devi Bhagvatam*, where the golden-skinned Parvati splits in two, becoming the dark Kalika and the fair Ambika—parallel goddesses riding off on their lion vahans or vehicles, to bring an end to demons. There is a similar story in *Vamana Purana*, where Devi Parvati splits herself into the fair-faced Gauri or the household goddess, and her fiercer counterpart Kaushiki, another form of Kali. In the literature of *Devi Mahatamya* of *Markandeya Purana*, Maa Kali emerges fully formed from

Durga's forehead in order to defeat the demon Raktabija, who was given the boon that every drop of his fallen blood would create another version of him, rendering him immortal. When the gods appealed to Kali, she finished him off by drinking all of his blood.

A more direct relationship between Devi Sati and Kali is the story of the how the Dus Mahavidyas came into being. Angered by her father Daksha's negligence towards her consort Shiva, Sati, through her anger, generated the ten magnificent goddesses of knowledge—the first of them being the ferocious Kali.

Kalighat, the region, is famous for its folk art devoted to the Devi and is also known as Kali Kshetra. The local folklore traces her worship to the wooded village of Gobindapur where she was frequented by hunters seeking a good prey. She was, in those days, 'guhya' or 'the hidden one'. When the temple was brought under the patronage of the landowning zamindar family of Sabarna Chaudhary, the class of its visitors was gentrified to include the city's elite and the upper middle class.

The temple opens in time for the 6 a.m. aarti and the closing prayers are conducted at 11 in the night. There is a reclining sculpture of Kali over her consort Shiva, where she is shown with a flaming golden tongue and three red eyes, holding a sickle and sculpted human head in her silver arms. The idol has a string of silver heads decorating her. There is an interesting custom pertaining to her annual ritual bath or holy dip called snan yatra, during which her priests are required to blindfold themselves before bathing her idol so as to not be blinded by her brilliance.

In the past, the deity was offered animal sacrifices, a custom frowned upon in modern society. Today, sacrificial goats are presented to the Goddess on certain occasions. Apart from the shrine dedicated to her Bhairava Nakuleshwar, there is also a shrine dedicated to Radha-Krishna within the Kalighat temple complex. The most important celebration here is Durga Puja, which is brought in with much fanfare and a special Kali Puja.

26

Jogadya Shakti Peetha
Kshirgram, West Bengal

Kssiiragraame Mahaamaayaa Bhairavah Kssiirakhannddakah |
Yugadyaa Saa Mahaamaayaa Dakssa-Anggussttham
Pado Mama ||26||

[At Kshiragram, the Mahamaya abides. The Bhairava there is called Kshirakhandaka whose name literally means a piece of kshira or condensed milk. The Mahamaya there is known as Yugadya whose name literally means 'one who begins the yuga'. There the daksha, or foot, has fallen.[8]]

Bardhaman district of West Bengal has earned its place in the historical narrative of India as a place of spirituality, where one finds in abundance terracotta temples, including the picturesque 108-Shiva temple. The temple earned this moniker because within its complex, one can find a total of 108 small Shiva temples, making an intricate vertical pattern. Each of these small temples has a representation of the deity, Shiva, within it. The local legends associated with the grand Shiva temple tell the story of Rani Bishnukumari, who received

---
[8]https://greenmesg.org/stotras/durga/shakti_peethas.php

divine guidance to construct such a temple of magnificence in her dreams. The temple is situated in the Nawabhat, which was once the place where the Pathans clashed with the Mughals. Today the temple comes to life for the celebrations of Shivratri, the divine night dedicated to Lord Shiva and his consort Devi Parvati. The whole place is lit up with lights and diyas in intricate designs and patterns. Not too far away are the Siddheshwari and the Sarbamangala temples, both ancient in their origins and dedicated to different aspects of Shakti.

It is in the eastern part of this district in the village of Kshirgram, also known locally as Khirgram, where we find the temple dedicated to Goddess Jogadya, an important tantric deity and an aspect of Shakti. The temple is considered a Shakti Peetha because this is the spot where Devi Sati's right toe, or as per alternative beliefs, her foot, fell.

The Devi Jogadya is deeply associated with Mahamaya, especially in the tantric tradition. Her name implies that she is the Goddess who births a new yuga, a Devi of time and creation. According to the *Devi Mahatamya* text, the primordial nature of the Universe, its ultimate reality, is believed to be feminine. This feminine energy is embodied in the Devi or the Mahamaya, meaning 'she who is the grand illusion' or 'she who possesses great deception'. In the Hindu tradition, the age of man is divided into yugas (an epoch or era in Hindu cosmology). In total, we have four yugas—Sata Yuga, Treta Yuga, Dvapara Yuga and Kali Yuga. The Goddess Jogadya is the Devi who brings about the new yuga in the cycle of man. In this respect, she holds the key to creation in the context of ages, the power to not only grant the ability to surpass the illusion of the world but also to spin the magnificent web of reality within which man lives.

In her Shakti Peetha in Kshirgram, she is accompanied by her consort in his Bhairava form, protecting her energy as Kshirakhandaka, whose name literally means 'a piece of sweet, condensed milk'. The form that is worshipped here is an idol, a figurine carved with great skill out of a plain black stone slab. The worship of the Devi peculiar to this temple is that the idol remains submerged in a nearby pond or kund for much of the duration of the year and is brought out only twice a year for a period of darshan.

Devotees visiting the temple have for long worshipped the Devi with traditional forms of worship like animal sacrifice, a practice, which in other temples, has evolved into a more acceptable, if somewhat more sophisticated, form of worship in modern times. Animals are traded for pumpkins, melons and watermelons. This manner of worship has stood the test of time in the Jogadya Shakti Peetha as it honours the destructive aspect of the Devi as a life force, as the one who gives and nurtures life. She creates and gives life with the same ease with which she takes it away and brings forth destruction of the physical form.

In Bengal, Durga is Mahamaya, a name earned because of her fierce personification as the destroyer of all demonic forms and attributes. Goddess Durga, who is Devi Mahatamya, Shakti, Mahamaya and Prakriti is the tri-fold goddess—the creator, the upholder or sustainer, and the destroyer—a cosmic role that draws her to the bij or seed of the universe. It is Jogadya who, in times when disorder threatens to disrupt the cosmos, intervenes to return order to creation, and eventually establishes the practise of Dharma.

Those who worship her, turn to her seeking a release from the illusion of life, for she is the one who guides man towards the ultimate truth, the nature of reality that extricates one from the cycle of death and rebirth.

27

Umakotilingeshwara Swamy or Godavari Tir Shakti Peetha
Rajahmundry, Andhra Pradesh

Gannddo Godaavarii-Tiire Vishveshii
Vishva-Maatrkaa ||45||
Dannddapaanni-Bhairavas-Tu
Vaama-Ganndde
Tu Raakinnii |
Bhairavo Vatsanaabhas-Tu Tatra
Siddhir-Na Samshayah ||46||[9]

[My ganga, or cheek, fell at Godavari Tir, where the Devi is known as Vishwesi, whose name literally means the 'Lord of the World', and she is Vishwamatrika, whose name means the 'Mother of the World'.
There the Bhairava is called Dandapani whose name literally means 'with a staff in the hand'; and with my left cheek falling there, the Devi is known as Rakini and the Bhairava is (also) called Vatsanabha, meaning 'with the navel like that of a child'.
At that place, there is no doubt about attaining Siddhi or spiritual accomplishments.]

---

[9]https://greenmesg.org/stotras/durga/shakti_peethas.php

In the east Godavari district of Andhra Pradesh is an old city which is known as Rajahmundry or Rajamahendravaram, a magnificent historical place which bore witness to the glorious rule of the Chalukya dynasty for 1,000 years. The language spoken in the state of Andhra Pradesh, Telugu, is believed to have been created in this city, and it has, over time, been a nodal point for modernism, as one of the first places in the colonial period to have seen the construction of a major river infrastructure in the form of a dam.

In Hindu scriptures, the river Godavari is revered second

only to the river Ganga. It originates in Nasik, Maharashtra, from where it flows towards the Bay of Bengal, splitting into two major streams from Rajahmundry, forming a delta. Up until this point, it is known as akhanda, unbroken. Rajahmundry, by the banks of its aquamarine waters, is where the Sri Umakotilingeshwara Swamy temple stands. It is also known as Godavari Tir, a lesser known Shakti Peetha but no less significant in its spiritual standing. According to local lore, this is where Devi Sati's cheeks plunged deep into the fertile earth, when Vishnu's Sudarshan Chakra cut through her lifeless body.

Umakotilingeshwara Temple
Photo: Creative Commons/Visurao4all

The significance of the Godavari as a river, in conjunction with the mythos of the Devi, is that it is one of the seven rivers across the Indian subcontinent venerated as holy and personified as the seven river deities or goddesses. The most popular of these legends usually pertain to Ganga. The stories of her inception have wound themselves into the narrative of the Hindu scriptures, forming a kind of blueprint for the mythos of the other, lesser rivers like Godavari and Narmada in the ancient texts.

There is a tale in the *Shiva Purana* about the great sage Gautama whose earnest prayers to Lord Shiva brought Godavari from the high peaks of the Brahmagiri mountain down to Earth to cast a web of worldly sins to allow man to live a life of fertility and auspiciousness. It is a story that bears remarkable similarity to the origin story of one other great river, Ganga or Bhagirathi, which was brought to earth through the efforts of King Bhagirath, for mankind to atone for its sins and live a righteous life. It is perhaps for this reason that Godavari or Gautami is also known as the Ganga of the South. In ancient times, it was common practice for the great rishis or sages to assist in manifesting rivers, their efforts a significant part of the literature surrounding the sacred geography of India or Bharat. Godavari is the river believed by many scholars to have split into a seven-stream delta, symbolizing the seven great sages or the Saptarishi, much in the way of the Ganga.

The Devi's mythos at the Godavari Shakti Peetha is strongly attached to the river Godavari itself; she then becomes the personification of the Goddess. One can trace sites of pilgrimage along the banks of the other sacred rivers. Godavari too has her historic sites of spiritual worship. These sacred teerthas stand in line with Godavari's trajectory and those who bathe in her waters attain spiritual enlightenment. The sages worshipping on her banks are granted Siddhis or spiritual accomplishments. Her waters bring fertility to the lands and as Vishwamatrika or the Mother of the World, she provides sustenance and life. It is believed locally that Mahadeva or Lord Shiva blessed the river with his constant presence as a companion and consort.

The temple of Sri Umakotilingeshwara Swamy becomes a prime example of the spiritual union of Shiva and the Devi at the Godavari Tir. Here, Devi Vishweshwari or Vishwamatrika blesses her devotees with her grace and as the lore goes, Gautama Rishi himself consecrated the Shiva lingam on the riverfront in a show of penance for his sins. In Puranic literature, we have the *Godavri Mahatamya,* or as it is alternatively known, *Gautami Mahatamya,* from the *Brahma Purana,* which tells us of the tale of Rishi Gautama and his quest to bring the river Godavari to Bharat. In it, eight pilgrimage sites are identified on the banks of the river where the Goddess' body parts fell; Rajahmundry thus becomes the site to attain the charan-sparsh of the Devi. With the presiding deities of the Godavari Tir being Shakti and Shiva, the festival of Shivratri is celebrated with much aplomb with pilgrims coming to her banks from all over India.

28

Panchasagar Shakti Peetha
Varanasi, Uttar Pradesh

Samhaara-[A]akhya Uurddha-Danto Devii-[A]nale Naaraayannii Shrucau |
Adho-Danto Mahaa-Rudro Vaaraahii Pan.casaagare ||39||[10]

[At Anala, my urdhva danta, or the upper row of teeth, fell. There the Devi is known as Narayani whose name literally means the 'power of Narayana', and the Bhairava there is called Samhara, meaning the one who destroys. At Panchasagara, my adho danta, or lower row of teeth, fell; there the Devi is known as Varahi whose name literally means 'with the face of the varaha or boar' and the Bhairava there is called Maharudra, whose name literally means 'one who is extremely terrible and fearsome'.]

The city of Kashi, Benaras, or Varanasi in contemporary times, was renowned in the canons of literature by Mark Twain's reference to it being 'older than history, older than tradition'. The great travellers and adventure seekers of history, those we credit with mapping out the world when not

---

[10] https://greenmesg.org/stotras/durga/shakti_peethas.php

much was known of it, described the magnificence of this jewel of an Indian city in all of its glory. For as long as its history has been recorded, Benaras has been a place where one could find the finest silk, rich brocades and textiles the quality of which one could find nowhere else in the world.

Right through the heart of the city flows India's sacred Ganga, which has given Benaras the status of one of the holiest cities in the Indian subcontinent. The banks of the Ganga, which are known locally as ghats, have in turn become hubs of spiritual activity, with rites of birth and death being carried out side by side. There are numerous temples of competing significance dotting the interwoven alleys and roads. On Manmandir Ghat not too far off from the well-known Dashashwamedh Ghat, one finds a temple that is dedicated to Goddess Varahi, revered as the Panchasagar Shakti Peetha. It is at the site of this temple that Devi Sati's lower jaw fell in the midst of Shiva's tandava.

The Varahi temple opens its gates at dawn only for two hours, and from that moment there is a mad rush of devotees and pilgrims visiting the Devi. What is unique to the Panchasagar Shakti Peetha is the manner in which the Devi is worshipped, where her association is stronger to Lord Vishnu than it is to her consort Lord Shiva. According to Puranic literature, Devi Varahi's mythos is intertwined with that of the sustainer Vishnu. Lord Vishnu, along with Brahma and Shiva, form the fundamental trinity of the godhead in the Hindu pantheon. This trinity is a means of dividing the three powers of the one supreme being—which are creation, sustenance and destruction—all of which stem from the primordial energy of one feminine force, Adi Shakti.

The Varaha avatara is one of Lord Vishnu's ten mahavataras. This form of Vishnu is the one with the head of a boar. Each of the avataras has a corresponding aspect of the Devi as its Shakti and the Varahi Devi is the shakti, or energy, of the Varaha avatara.

The set of seven Mother Goddesses or Saptamatrikas embody

the feminine counterparts of the devas, their Shakti, as per the text of *Devi Mahatamya*. They appeared during Durga's battle with Chanda and Munda and helped her fight, and later danced in wild exuberance when she was victorious. These Saptamatrikas, once they had taken form, remained female counterparts and were accordingly attached to the respective devas—Brahmani with Brahma, Maheshwari with Shiva, Vaishnavi with Vishnu, Varahi with Varaha, Narasimhi with Narasimhan, Indrani from Indra, and Kaumari with Kartikeya.

In Benaras, many attribute Varahi's creation from Vishnu to Shiva. And yet in a popular story, Varahi is described as one of the Chausath yoginis, or 64 yoginis, that Shiva sent to Benaras. According to an alternative mythos, Varahi was believed to have assisted Varaha in his efforts to save the Earth when the demon Hiranyaksha tried to drown it in the cosmic ocean. The Devi in this aspect is depicted as being seated on the snout of Varaha's wild boar head, as his tusks fish the Earth out of the deep waters of the ocean.

Varahi is depicted with the head of a sow and is usually adorned in a red sari, decked in jewels. She offers her protection against evil, and in most representations, is seen carrying a disc-like weapon similar to the Sudarshan Chakra, much like Vishnu. She also holds a conch shell, the sound of which signifies auspicious beginnings, a sword in her hand, and various agricultural implements symbolizing fertility and sustenance. Her vahan—a lion, a wild boar or a buffalo—is depicted differently, based on the sects worshipping her, perhaps marking her association to Durga as Mahishasuraa Mardini. In some depictions, her vahan is also represented as the mythical bird Garuda. During the festival of Navratas, which comes twice a year, pilgrims and worshippers come in hoards to the Panchasagar Shakti Peetha to pay their respects to the Devi.

29

Devi Danteshwari Shakti Peetha
Bastar, Chhattisgarh

Iishvara Uvaaca |
Maatah Paraatpare Devi Sarva-
Jnyaanamayi-[I]ishvari |
Kathyataam Me Sarva-Piittha-
Shakti-Bhairava-Devataah ||1||

[Ishwara said: The Mother who is the Paratpara (superior to the best), who is the Devi having all knowledge within her, told me about all the Shakti Peethas along with the Bhairava Devatas (Shiva)[11].]

The Shakti Peethas transcend Puranic classical thought and enter the domain of the vernacular and the margins. One such site of the Shakti Peetha is in the tribal belt of Central India in the newly formed state of Chhattisgarh—the Devi Danteshwari Peetha.

Deep in the heart of the forested tribal belt of Chhattisgarh in Central India, stands the historic site of Maa Danteshwari in Dantewada, a 600-year-old Shakti Peetha. It is on its hallowed

---

[11]https://greenmesg.org/stotras/durga/shakti_peethas.php

grounds that Devi Sati's teeth or 'dant', are believed to have fallen. Devi Danteshwari is a major deity in the district of Bastar where Dantewada falls. However, her image as Danteshwari is not local to the place. The Devi's worship was brought to Bastar by the Kakatiyas, who were Chandravanshi Rajput rulers of the region between the 12th and 14th centuries CE. The reverence to the Devi has been a common practice among Rajput rulers across the Indian subcontinent. Her aspects of justice, sustenance, fierceness and power were qualities which were held in great esteem by the ruling class. Devi Danteshwari was thus the kuldevi, or the dynasty deity, for the Kakatiyas, who brought her with them when they conquered the thick forests of Chakrakot from Warangal in present day Telangana. Bastar, which is the site of the temple, lies in the land which is on the confluence of rivers Shankini and Dankini.

The original temple was consecrated by King Annamadeva and the community followed in his footsteps in worshipping the Devi; her devotees went on to be called jogis. A cultural practice regarding the Goddess's worship that is particular to this region is that historically, the descendants of Bastar's kings become the high priests of the Peetha of Devi Danteshwari. There is a popular local tale which tells of an incident when King Annamadeva was on the run from invaders coming in from Warangal. He prayed to Devi Danteshwari for her protection and the Devi came to him in a dream with the promise that he should begin walking and wherever he went, she would follow. The land they both covered together would go on to become his new kingdom. As the tale goes, the Devi had only one condition in lieu of offering her protection, which was that if he turned around, she would leave him at that very moment. At the point of confluence of Shankini and Dankini, when the sounds of her anklets disappeared because she had stepped into the water, the king, because of his burning curiosity, turned around to look, thus setting the boundary of his new kingdom. It was the immense influence of King Annamadeva because of which the sacred sites for the worship of Devi Danteshwari came up in Jagdalpur, Bade Dongar, Katekalyan and Barsur.

The Devi Danteshwari Shakti Peetha in Bastar, as we see it today, is a humble structure made of wood, with a column before it, sitting atop which is Garuda, the vahan of Lord Vishnu. Within the structure sits the idol of the Goddess, carved beautifully out of a slab of black stone. The temple architecture is inspired by the Dravidian aesthetic. Beside the innermost sanctum sanctorum that includes the garbhagriha housing the Devi, there is a mahamandap, a mukhyamandap and a sabhamandap.

As the royal Goddess, the offerings made to Danteshwari as part of her worship include a prasada of milk, rice and clarified butter or ghee, and she is venerated with the fresh blossoms that grow aplenty in the region. The district of Bastar is known for many vibrant festivals that are held all year round. The madhais, or special fairs which were established by the royal family mostly in the time of the colder months when several rural deities were worshipped, are to this day a big draw for the Devi's worship, who takes a prime spot among them. Each autumn, Bastar holds the festival of Dussehra which lasts for 75 days, beginning from the months of monsoon and rising to a crescendo with the finale of Vijayadashmi. It is believed that King Annamadeva used to partake in the newly harvested crop only after making its offering to Devi Danteshwari on the day of Dussehra.

The celebrations of Dussehra in the district of Bastar uniquely surround the worship of the Devi rather than Lord Rama. Danteshwari is thus celebrated as Durga or Mahishasuraa Mardini, the primordial divine energy who was called upon by the gods when evil brimmed over into the world in the form of the buffalo-headed Mahishasura, wreaking havoc across the three loks. In the tribal area of Jagdalpur, the communities step out in large numbers, cheering alongside the procession of the local deities led by the Devi. Mahua, the locally sourced liquor, is consumed and it is a time of economic abundance as handcrafted wares of tribal communities are displayed for sale. The chariots which carry the local deities and the Devi from Dantewada were inspired by the procession that is taken from the Jagannath temple in Puri. The custom of wheeling gods through the town in fact dates back to the 15th century when King Purshottam Deo had witnessed a similar rath yatra in Puri and had believed or experienced it as Jagannath himself going through the town bestowing his blessings upon the people who encountered him, giving him the honourable position of the rathpati. It was this belief and tradition that was brought to Bastar and became part of the ritual lore of Devi Danteshwari.

30

Srisailam Shakti Peetha
Srisailam, Andhra Pradesh

*Shriishaile Ca Mama Griivaa Mahaalakssmiis-Tu Devataa |
Bhairavah Sambaraanando Desho Desho Vyavasthitah*[12]

[At Srisailam, my griva, or neck, fell, and the Devata, implying the Devi in this context, there is known as Mahalakshmi. The Bhairava is called Sambarananda whose name literally means the bliss that comes from the restraint of meditation. She is the one who abides in every place.]

The *Shakti Peetha Stotram* by Adi Sankaracharya mentions Srisailam as one of the 18 principal Mahapeethas or the major Shakti Peethas. According to him, the Devi here is Brahmarambika. In the legend of Sati, this is the spot where the Devi's neck fell. She is also known as Mahalakshmi. The Srisailam Shakti Peetha temple complex is in the town of Srisailam in the district of Kurnool, Andhra Pradesh. It is known also as the Brahmaramba Mallikarjuna Swamy Varla Devasthanam. Not too far from the Srisailam reservoir, on the river Krishna, the temple complex stands overlooking the hilly terrain called Sriparvatha, part of the Nallamalai range that surrounds it.

---

[12]https://greenmesg.org/stotras/durga/shakti_peethas.php

The local population believes the following episode from the *Devi Mahatamya* text: The Goddess turned herself into a bee or a bhramar, in order to slay the demon Arunasura. This is where her name, Brahmaramba, came from and this is why it is attached to this particular Shakti Peetha. The Bhairava who protects the Peetha is known as Samvaranand, and the temple is equally famous for this form of Shiva as it is for the Devi. In fact it is even considered to be one of the jyotirlingams. The *Skanda Purana* carries a tale about Princess Chandravathi, believed to be from the Chandragupta Dynasty, who discovered the jyotirlingam. The princess had taken refuge in the mountains of Srisailam from the improper advances of her father. While wandering in the forests of this hilly region, she happened to come across a cow pouring its milk on a rock shaped in the form of a lingam. That night, Lord Shiva came to her in a dream, explaining how the rock was a manifestation of him. When Chandravathi awoke, she went about consecrating a temple around the lingam and led a daily worship of the lingam with jasmine flowers, known locally as Mallika flowers, thus giving the temple the name Mallikarjuna.

In *Durga Saptashati*, the Devi or Mahadevi is described as the supreme power behind all time, wealth and wisdom of existence. She is Mahakali, Mahalakshmi and Mahasaraswati. As we delve deeper into her, the Shakti of her aspects, we discover that as Mahasaraswati, she is the Goddess of divine knowledge, as Mahalakshmi she is the Goddess of supreme love and delight, and as Mahakali she is the Goddess of supreme strength and destruction. This is the manifestation of the Devi's tripartite role which goes into creating the universe, preserving it, and when the time comes, dissolving it. The most commonly held interpretation of the Devi's tripartite form associates her with her male godhead counterpart, with Mahalakshmi being the consort to Vishnu, assisting him in his role as the maintainer of the universe alongside Brahma and Mahasaraswati as creators, and Shiva and Mahakali as the dissolvers. These three functions

Srisailam Temple
Photo: Creative Commons/Saisumanth532

become part of the Devi's Dus Mahavidyas.

Inside the temple one finds the idol of Brahmaramba, sitting atop the Sriparvatha. There is a sacred diagram of concentric circles on a round piece of stone—the Sri Chakra. The Sri Chakra is widely known as the yantra of Tripura Sundari, a seat of her power as per the tantric traditions. Tripura Sundari is the Goddess who is closely associated with the triad of creation, sustenance and destruction. This is possibly the reason why her yantra is present in the temple. There are local stories explaining the presence of the yantra which surround the great sage Adi Sankaracharya himself. It is said that when Sankaracharya was here, he had to face a rather angry and violent Brahmaramba Devi and as a way of placating her anger and soothing her, he created the yantra and placed it beside her.

Sriparvatha as a location of this powerful yantra and as an abode of the Devi is also known colloquially as Srigiri. Sri is the alternate name given to Goddess Lakshmi, and is tied closely to her identity as the supreme Mahalakshmi. As Sri, she is the bestower of wealth. Adi Sankaracharya, who also composed the Kanaka Dhara Stotram in honour of Sri, described her power to relieve even an impoverished woman of her destitution. The utterance of her very name is associated with the material side of existence.

In the Sriparvatha temple complex, one finds sculptures of Gajalakshmi adorning the main temple structure. As Lakshmi emerged from the cosmic ocean of milk which both the devas and the asuras had been churning so that they may receive the nectar of life, elephants or gajas bestowed an offering of water over her with their trunks, giving her the monicker of Gajalakshmi. The showering of the water, according to David Kinsley's *Tantric Visions of the Divine*, has two connotations—one is in hope of good rain and fertility, and the other is representational of her royal stature, since elephants are a symbol of royalty.

Mahalakshmi, as many scholars state, is independent of Lord

Vishnu. She is depicted much like Durga—not as a beautiful Goddess seated on a lotus, but as a warrior riding atop a lion. This depiction is the source of the Brahmaramba idol at Sriparvatha, which is depicted in the image of Mahishasuramardini, the fearsome aspect of Durga. She has eight hands which hold weapons of war like the sword, bow and arrows, and a mace, and is shown killing a buffalo demon with her holy trident or trishul.

Primarily a Vaishnav geography, the Srisailam Peetha is dedicated to the Devi and Shiva. Sriparvatha is compared as such to Mount Kailash, the Himalayan abode of Shiva and Parvati, and as one of the jyotirlingams of India, it is believed to appear as a divine light in the sacred geography of India. The temple complex is lined with shrines and mandapas such as the Nandimandapa dedicated to Shiva's bull, the Uma-Maheshwara shrine, and the Sahasralinga which is the 1,000-lingam shrine. The mandapas are all adorned with exquisite carvings of episodes from Puranic texts.

31

Nandikeshwari Shakti Peetha
Birbhum, West Bengal

Haara-Paato Nandipure Bhairavo Nandikeshvarah |
Nandinii Saa Mahaa-Devii Tatra Siddhim-Avaapnuyaat

[At Nandipura, my hara (necklace) fell. There the Bhairava is called Nandikeshwara (literally meaning the Lord of Nandi). And the Mahadevi (Great Goddess) is known as Nandini (literally meaning one who gives joy). There, one attains Siddhi (spiritual accomplishments).][13]

The lush greenery of Birbhum district of West Bengal enriches the spiritual abode of the Supreme Goddess. From the raw notes of the Baul minstrels, to the flourishing art schools of Shantiniketan, the district is further enriched by the spiritual movement of the Shakta sect.

There is a Shakta trail for the pilgrims here: the Phullara temple in Labpur, the Tarapith and Kankalitala Peetha in Bolpur, and the temple of Mahishasuramardini at Bakreshwar, a similar distinct town known for its Shakti worship and located in the industrial town of Sainthia. The Nandini Devi Shakti Peetha in Birbhum, popularly known as Sainthia's Nandikeshwari temple,

---

[13]https://greenmesg.org/stotras/durga/shakti_peethas.php

is close to the banks of the river Mayurakshi where, according to the legend of the *Devi Purana*, the Goddess Sati's necklace fell.

At Sainthia, respect is paid to Goddess Parvati in her benevolent form as Nandini or Nandikeshwari. The object of worship is a boulder that has turned red through the ritual of offering vermilion, a symbol of holy matrimony in Hinduism, closely associated with the Goddess' worship. She is depicted here with three eyes. The Devi is one with her divine consort Shiva. Nandi, who is Shiva's bull mount and a signature element in his worship all through his folkloric mythology and imagery, defines this union between Parvati, as Nandini, and her beloved Shiva. Nandi plays a crucial part here as not simply an emblem of Shiva but also a representation of agriculture, fertility and sustenance. Nandikeshwari thus evokes the aspect of the life-giving principles of creation. There are similar aspects of her such as Annapurna, the Goddess of bountiful produce; Mangala Chandi, the Goddess of domesticity; and Rathai Chandi, a similar benevolent form of Parvati. Nandikeshwari is one of the many names of the divine Goddess or the Devi, as she is worshipped on the fertile belt of West Bengal because of her creative ability to bring about life. Nandini Devi is also known as Girinandini, the daughter of the mountains, which was one of the first names given to Devi Parvati, and is believed to have been born to the Himalayas or Himavan.

There are many episodes from the Devi's life on earth, her many aspects, which come alive in the sculptures in the Nandikeshwari temple, including the depiction of the Devi through her ten knowledge aspects or Mahavidyas. The imagery mostly belongs to the ancient iconography of the divine Goddess. Her ten powerful forms of intelligence were born out of her in different moments of provocation or challenge, when she was faced by a battle between good and evil, mostly in a literal battlefield, before an army of demons, but also in the spiritual field of the atman's pursuit of the parmatman.

In West Bengal, the Devi is worshipped all year round as the primary deity. However, her mythology has evolved from a Ramayana story called 'Akala Bodhana,' meaning 'untimely worship' from which the rituals of the Navratras arise. Traditionally, there is a special ceremony conducted in honour of Goddess Durga as the demon-slaying Mahishasuraa Mardini, observed in the months of spring. As Rama was on his way to Lanka to fight against Ravana in order to rescue his wife Sita, he got to know that Ravana had the blessings of Durga herself and to win against him, it was imperative for Rama to appease Durga. In a magnificent havana to appease the Goddess, Rama arranged to have 108 lotuses presented to the Devi along with his prayers. When he reached out for the final 108th lotus, he found that it was missing. To complete his puja, Lord Rama began to carve out one of his own eyes which resembled the lotus to place at the Devi's altar. At this moment, the Devi appeared and stopped him. The Devi, pleased, blessed him with grace for victory and thus Rama went unfettered into war with Ravana, establishing the rule of good in the land of Lanka.

In Nandikeshwari, in the months of autumn during the Navratras, the entire temple complex comes to life in celebration of the Goddess' strength and victory over demonic forces. At this time, even the Goddess' gentler form as an aspect of food and nourishment is recognized for its fierce appearance on the battlefield.

32

Uma Shakti Peetha
Mithila, Bihar

Namah sivabhyam navayauvanabhyam
Parasparaslistavapurdharabhyam
Nagendrakanyavrsaketanabhyam
Namo namah sankaraparvatibhyam[14]

[At Mithila, the Devi is known as Uma. There my vama skanda, or left shoulder, fell; and the Bhairava here is called Mahodara, whose name literally means 'the one with the large belly'.]

—UMAMAHESWARA STOTRAM[15]

In the northern region of Bihar is the ancient city of Mithila, which spreads across the geographical expanse of contemporary national borders into the country of Nepal. It is a place of great significance as in the Ramayana, Mithila was the birthplace of Rama's queen, Devi Sita. The newborn Sita, according to Puranic lore, was accidentally discovered by her adoptive father, Raja Janaka, as he was ploughing the field during a particularly strenuous season of drought.

In Mithila, in the town of Darbhanga, close to the Indo-

---

[14]https://greenmesg.org/stotras/durga/shakti_peethas.php
[15]https://stotranidhi.com/en/uma-maheshwara-stotram-in-english/

Nepal border, is a Shakti temple where it is believed that Devi Sati's left shoulder or vama skanda, fell, making Mithila a bed of immense spiritual power. This Shakti Peetha is dedicated to Goddess Uma, a benevolent form of Parvati. The temple complex has a pillared courtyard and lattice details on the walls of the shrine which is kept as a simple white structure. At Mithila, Goddess Uma is worshipped alongside her divine consort Lord Shiva. To this day, devotees pray to both Uma and Shiva since these prayers hold the promise of bringing marital bliss and a peaceful domestic co-existence in the lives of married couples. The idols worshipped in the temple show the two deities perched on an obscure rock. Shiva is known here in his Bhairava avatara as Mahodara or Maheshwara and Devi Uma as Mahadevi.

Most Puranic and Vedic texts elaborate and stress on the role played by the Devi as the power and force of creation. Over centuries, the identity of the Goddess has evolved into and in accordance with her various aspects or representational roles. Each of her aspects is used interchangeably in popular lore when speaking of her as the divine companion and consort of Lord Shiva. At its greatest heights, this union is represented in the form of the Ardhanarishwara avatara. However there are many ways to consider this partnership. The first is as the co-householder, the Goddess lures Shiva towards the life of a householder. She is the mother of his children and her role in the mythology was, to a large extent, of one who introduces this ash-covered, tiger hide-wearing ascetic to the joys of domestic life. The Devi was once represented as the gentle, dark-skinned Goddess but perhaps in line with social norms of beauty or mainstream imagination, her darkness was said to have separated from her to create another aspect of her—Kaushiki or the dark-skinned one—leaving Uma or Gauri as the beautiful golden-skinned wife of Mahadeva.

Another Shakt tradition has its own interpretation. It is believed that Shiva without Shakti is a shava, or corpse. It is the Mahadevi who breathes life into Shiva or Mahadeva. It is Mahalakshmi who gives the shakti to Vishnu to sustain the universe, and it is Mahasaraswati who unveils the secret of the universe, the knowledge of the supreme, for Brahma. These three defined images of the Devi are the origins of the triad of godheads that are Brahma, Vishnu and Maheshwara.

When Durga was called upon to go into battle with the demon Mahishasura, her entire being was created by the unified prayers of the devas, the male deities, who represent various elements, but instead of becoming an entity dependent on their powers for her own existence, her strength goes beyond them all and is considered to be the primary consciousness from which everything begins and ends.

This temple is often confused with the sprawling, magnificent Ram Janaki temple in Janakpur in Nepal, because of the intersection between the tales of the Devi and the tales from Ramayana, especially with episodes of Rama's havana before waging war on Lanka. The fact that Devi Sita is a Goddess in her own right blurs the already fuzzy lines between Devi worship and Sita's worship. According to a popular belief in the region, there are three alternate locations of the Mithila Shakti Peetha, and one of them is said to be the Vanadurga temple in Janakpur. There is also a Durga or Vanadurga temple in Uchchaith village in Madhubani, also considered the Mithila Shakti Peetha, and a shrine in Samastipur, in the state of Bihar as well. It is however widely accepted that the Uma Shakti Peetha itself is the Mithila Shakti Peetha.

33

Tara Tarini Shakti Peetha
Ganjam, Odisha

Taaraa Ca Taarinnii Devii Naaga-Munndda-Vibhuussitaa |
Lalaj-Jihvaa Niila-Varnnaa Brahma-Ruupa-Dharaa Tathaa ||
Naaga-Ancita-Kattii Devii Niila-Ambara-Dharaa Paraa ||

[I meditate on Devi Tara. Tara who is Tarini Devi, the Goddess who makes us cross the Samsara; who is Naga-Munda-Vibhushita, the one who is adorned with the heads of demons, who has a fearful appearance with Lala-Jihva, the one with a lolling tongue; who is Nila-Varna, the one with a blue complexion; who is Brahma-Rupa-Dhara, the Brahman in an embodied form; who is Naga-Ancita-Kati Devi, the Devi around whose hip are curled serpents; who is of transcendental nature and Nila-Ambara-Dhara, the one who is clothed by the blue sky.]

—TARA STOTRAM[16]

The old Ganjam district of southern Odisha stands on the solitary, idyllic banks of River Rushikulya, 30 km north of the coastal town of Behrampur. It is here where one finds a temple dedicated to the Devi called Tara Tarini Peetha.

---

[16] https://greenmesg.org/stotras/tara/tara_stotram.php

According to Adi Sankaracharya's *Shakti Peetha Stotram*, the Tara Peetha is considered to be an Adi Peetha, which means that it is one of the four most important Shakti Peethas within the Shakta sect. According to the Devi's mythos, it is believed that this is the spot where Sati's stan khand, or breasts, fell, and the temple which stands on the modest hillock is named Tara Tarini after its patron twin goddesses.

Local legend speaks of a Brahman priest called Vasu Praharaja, who had adopted two young girls who were lost. He took great care of them but one day the twins simply disappeared. Vasu Praharaja looked everywhere for them but he couldn't find them, leaving him to mourn the disappearance of his daughters. That night, they appeared to him in a dream, revealing their true self—they were none other than Adi Shakti herself. Upon their direction, Praharaja built a small shrine on the hilltop where the temple stands today, consecrating its power with a ritual yagna.

Devi Tara and Devi Tarini are counted among the Dus Mahavidyas, representational deities or aspects of the Goddess who were born out of her primordial energy as the supreme knowledge. Each one makes an independent appearance in the origin myths of the Mahavidyas. In the *Devi Bhagvata Purana*, when the Mahadevi is battling the demon Durgama—victory against whom gave her the name Durga—Devi Tarini was the second Mahavidya who emerged from within her, after Kali, to join her army. Similarly in a tale from the *Mahabhagvata Purana*, there is an episode when Sati, who is upset at not being invited to her father's yagna, starts a row with her husband Shiva on attending it nonetheless. When Shiva is about to leave, out of annoyance, Sati's ten forms emerge from within her, surrounding him and making it impossible for him to leave. Tara is the second of these celestial forms to appear right after Devi Kali. In many accounts in fact, Tara is often identified as Devi Kali because of the depiction of her fearsome form.

In the state of Odisha, Devi Tarini has deep roots in the tribal ritual practices of the region. For a time, she was the royal deity of the Keonjhar region, which is at some distance from the Ganjam temple site towards the north. In contemporary times, the Devis, Tara and Tarini, are worshipped on the Rushikulya bank as the ishta-devata, or main family deity, of most of the households across the state.

Many scholars believe that Goddess Tara is a result of the Buddhist influence on the Devi's original form, as part of Emperor Ashoka's battle of Kalinga and his adoption of Buddhism. Kalinga covered what is the present-day Ganjam district and there is an edict of King Ashoka not too far off from the Tara Tarini temple site, at the ancient fort ruins of Jaugada. The name that is given to Devi Tarini is interpreted widely by scholars as the one who safely ferries her devotees across the ocean of samsara, the illusionary land that provides the experience of living and that is full of bondage. The Tara Tarini temple of Ganjam district is thus an important stop for those embarking on this voyage both in ancient times and today. The temple is close to the port, and is a metaphor for a spiritual journey, which becomes all too real here, with sailors making a stop at the temple before setting out. The strong belief in the power of the Tara Tarini Peetha led to the naming of a ship going on a world tour in 2017, with an all-women crew of the Indian Navy, as the INSV Tarini. As Tarini, the Devi is also the guardian of all sea-farers.

To reach the Tara Tarini Peetha, her devotees have to climb 1,000 steps upto the hilltop where her shrine stands. There, one is welcomed by two stones bedecked in gold and silver as symbols of the Goddess. One finds figurines besides the two stone sculptures, which are the chalanti pratima or movable idols that are taken out for yatras and processions during festivals and as part of the rituals. The idols are washed with the water from the Rushikulya, in a bathing ceremony known as Majana, done

Tara Tarini Temple
Photo: Creative Commons/Nayansatya

twice a day just prior to the temple aarti, after which they are covered in sandalwood and turmeric paste. The prasada given to the Goddess is a simple offering of sweets, fruits and khichdi.

In the traditional Chaitra month that is March–April, during the celebrations of Navratras which is a sacred period of Devi worship, on all four Tuesdays of the month, the devotees of the Goddess bring their children to the temple for their first ritual haircut, or mundan.

34

Mangala Gauri Shakti Peetha
Gaya, Bihar

Sarva Mangala Mangalye
Sive Sarvartha Sadhike
Saranye Trayambike Gauri
Narayani Namostute

[Salutations to you, O Narayani, who is the auspiciousness in all the auspicious, auspiciousness herself, complete with all the auspicious attributes, and who fulfils all the objectives of the devotees—Purusharthas: Dharma, Artha, Kama and Moksha; who is the giver of refuge, with three eyes and a shining face; salutations to you, O Narayani.]

—DEVI MAHATAMYA[17]

The city of Gaya in Bihar evokes the lore of the enlightened one, Shakyamuni Buddha. It is a shraadh Peetha, a place which is dedicated to offering prayers and obeisances to one's ancestors. The river Falgu runs through the heart of the city and is believed to be cursed by Sita as per a tale in the Ramayana, in which the river turned hostile as a witness to her propitiating Rama's ancestors amidst the ritual of pind daan.

---

[17]https://greenmesg.org/stotras/durga/sarvamangala_mangalye.php

Today the river Falgu is a seasonal river, winding itself around the Shakti Peetha of Mangala Gauri, a temple perched on top of the Mangalagauri Hill. The site of the temple of Mangala Gauri is not only associated with stories of ancestral worship stemming from the Ramayana but also refers to an episode from the Mahabharata when the Pandava brothers come to the temple and the banks of the river Falgu to perform shraadh to their ancestors while on their vanvas. Bhimvedi, the Bhima temple, is where this Pandava brother is believed to have kneeled in the midst of the shraadh ceremony.

The Goddess here is known as Sarvamangala, the devoted spouse of Shiva. It is believed that Devi Sati's breasts fell here, making it one such site which lays claim to the same anga or body part belonging to another site. The Devi is worshipped in accordance to the representation of this particular body part, with devotees paying their obeisance to two rotund stones. The Mangala Gauri temple is also known as a Maa Peetha, one of the main sites listed in Adi Sankaracharya's text, which is a compilation of the important sites of Shakti worship in the Indian subcontinent. The Devi as Durga or Dakshina Kali is worshipped alongside her consort Shiva, venerated in their Uma-Maheshwara form. Their union is depicted in the sculptures dotting the temple, but one also can worship them independently in their shrine, with one for Shiva at the foot of the hill where he exists in Parpita Maheshwara form and the Devi atop the hill as Mangala Gauri.

Each of the 108 names of the Devi ascribes her with certain qualities specific to her different aspects. Mangala Gauri is thus the life-giving Mother Goddess who births and nurtures children and is creation itself. She interlaces with Gauri, Jaganmatri, Vishwaroopini, Maheshwari, Mahamaya, Parvati, Ambika, Kaumari, Kalyani, Annapurna, Nirmala and Saubhagyadayi. In this mythos of the Devi's 108 names, Gauri is often perceived as the all-pervasive Devi when she is ten years of age. In *Devi:*

The Goddesses of India, David Kinsley writes that 'In the Vamana Puranan, Parvati is called Kali because of her dark complexion. When Parvati hears Shiva use this name she takes offence and does various austerities to rid herself of her dark skin. After she succeeds in this, she is renamed as Gauri or the golden one.' Thus, Gauri is the ultimate embodiment of spiritual, aesthetic and marital beauty.

Then there is her fiery image as Mahishasuramardini, which according to the *Devi Bhagvata Purana*, is the title given to the Devi upon her victory against the buffalo demon Mahishasura. Etymologically, Mahisasuramardini means 'beyond reach'; she is thus the 'forceful' form of the Goddess and is considered an echo of the female-warrior's fierce virginal autonomy.

As the river fills up during the months of monsoon, it is a special period for prayers and the worship of the Devi. Every Tuesday, which is a day particularly auspicious in Devi worship, women fast and perform a small ceremony for the longevity of their married lives through the well-being of their husbands. Mangala Gauri is honoured in her shrine with bangles, vermilion, fruits and sweets—some of her favourite fares. Her image in the temple is both a photograph of the Devi and a sculpture dipped in milk and water, wrapped in a red cloth, and decorated with henna and kohl, the symbols of married women.

35

Shivani Devi Shakti Peetha

Ramagiri, Uttar Pradesh

Shonna-[A]akhyaa Bhadrasenastu
Narmada-[A]akhye Nitambakah |S
Raamagirau Stanaanyan.-Ca Shivaanii
Canndda-Bhairavah[18]

[At the place called Narmada, where my nitamba (buttocks) fell, the Devi is called Sona, whose name literally means 'reddish', and the Bhairava there is called Bhadrasena. At Ramagiri, my stana, or breasts, fell. There the Devi is known as Shivani, whose name literally means the consort of Shiva, and the Bhairava there is called Chanda, whose name literally means one who is fierce.]

In the lush green landscape of Central India that is watered by the glory of the Mandakini, is the city of Chitrakoot known for its famed association with Lord Rama's vanvas in the Ramayana. This idyllic place has been identified as Kalidasa's Ramagiri, the home of the great poet, and lies across the two states of Uttar Pradesh and Madhya Pradesh. On the side of the border that falls in Uttar Pradesh is the Shakti Peetha dedicated

---

[18] https://greenmesg.org/stotras/durga/shakti_peethas.php

to Goddess Shivani, a benevolent aspect of the Devi, and her Bhairava here is Chanda, the one who is fierce. It is one of the contested spots where Devi Sati's breasts fell, and it is believed locally that at this Peetha, the Devi's right breast fell.

Shivani, as her name implies, is a gentler form of Devi Parvati, her identity strongly embedded into her form as a consort of Shiva. There are few instances in which Devi Parvati appears independent of her husband. She is most often seen seated beside him as his Shakti. When we hear tales of battle and victory, it is in her fiercer aspect as Kali or Durga.

However, this in no way reduces her significance, for according to Puranic Hindu myths, the reason that Parvati had to take form and experience the maya of the world after the passing of Sati was because it was she and only she who could lure Shiva away from a life of asceticism towards a life of domesticity as a householder. Shiva had to participate through his marriage into the circle of worldly affairs rather than wander forever in the forest, wild and aloof as an ascetic. There was a desperate need for balance to be restored in the universe, a goal only attainable by the gentle aspect of the Devi, as the beautiful maiden who would wed Shiva. As Sati, Parvati or Shivani, she is the maiden, the wife and the mother, who channels Shiva's ascetic energy positively towards creation in the affairs of the world.

As Shiva's Shakti, Shivani is associated with certain philosophical attributes which link her to the creative process of the cosmos. As a determined devotee, she is the spiritual aspirant who performs the most strenuous austerities in order to attain her spiritual union with Shiva who represents the parmatman. It is in fact Parvati's or Shivani's asceticism, devotion and spiritual curiosity which attract the great lord Shiva to her. There are episodes in Puranic texts where Shiva or an agent of Shiva set this devotion of the Goddess as examples for those who intend to follow her path in the eras to come. Each time the Devi succeeds, a tale is transcribed as a lesson in spiritual attainment.

The worship of Devi Shivani continues to take her place alongside her divine consort, Mahadeva. It is she who gives direction to his potent ascetic power, and who accompanies him in the creation of new forms of civilized life through literature, poetry, dance, music, yoga, spiritual enlightenment and more. She is the medium through which the many forms of knowledge are brought into the world, and it is she who is considered to be the gatekeeper of all the secrets of creation.

36

Sharada Devi Shakti Peetha

Maihar, Madhya Pradesh

Ya kundendu tushara haara dhavala,
Ya shubhra vastravrita
Ya veena vara danda mandithakara,
Ya shwetha padmaasana
Ya brahmachyuthaha shankara
Prabrithibhi devai, sada poojitha
Samaam paatu saraswathi bhagavathi

[One who is white as a 'kund' flower, the moon, icy snow and a pearl necklace; one who is adorned in pure white clothing; one who is beautiful as she holds the Veena; one who is seated on a white lotus; one for whom Brahma, Achyuta (Vishnu) and Shankara (Shiva) sing constant praises, and who removes all obstacles... O divine (Bhagavati) Saraswati, dispel my ignorance.]

—SIDDHA SARASWATI STOTRAM[19]

The small, bustling cosy town of Maihar, situated in the Satna district of Madhya Pradesh is a robust Shakti Peetha. On the towering heights of the Trikuta hill is the unassuming white spire of a beautiful temple structure dedicated

---
[19] http://sanskritslokas.com/saraswati-mantra/page-1.html

to Sharada Devi. Devotees who come to pay their respects to the Goddess participate in a hefty trek of 1,063 steps to the hilltop, or for those older in age, the ropeway, for the well-earned darshan of the Devi. The town, Maihar, received its name from the pind of the Devi which fell upon its hallowed grounds—its name literally meaning 'mother's necklace'—for this was the spot where Devi Sati's necklace landed.

The image of Sharada Maa is made of panchdhatu, or a mélange of five metals, viz. gold, silver, bronze, copper and iron. In this aspect she is most closely associated with Devi Saraswati, or Mahasaraswati, the sacred river from the Vedas believed to have dried up over the ages. She stands armed with her veena, a book in one hand and a pot of honey or water (the nectar of knowledge) in the other. She is the Goddess of the spoken sound—speech and music—an extension of her domain of learning, wisdom and intellectual discrimination. Devi Sharada, much like Devi Saraswati, is mostly depicted dressed in pure tones of all white or yellow. In her book, *The Book of Devi*, Bulbul Sharma writes 'Saraswati is considered as the muse of the poets, artists, and musicians, and she is invoked by them whenever artistic excellence is desired. Even the gandharvas, who are the celestial singers and dancers, pray to her for inspiration before they sing or dance in the presence of the devas.'

Home of Ustad Allauddin Khan, the high priest of the Maihar gharana and guru of some of the finest maestros of Indian classical music, the temple of Sharada Maa is an inclusive site for religion and music.

In the choice of attire for the Devi, when we consider her dress in white or yellow, we are compelled to think of the significance of the colours—yellow as the colour symbolic of agni is considered pure enough to burn the illusion of the world, or the ego; white is a colour that takes on nothing external, exists wholly in its own domain, power or shakti. These imply that Devi Sharada is self-composed, standing tall in her sublime shakti.

Sharada Temple
Photo: Creative Commons/L.R. Burdak

In Maihar, there is a shrine that is dedicated to Adi Sankaracharya, standing beside the innermost sanctum of Sharada Devi. Adi Sankaracharya, the learned sage from Kerala from the 8th century and a Devi Bhakt, compiled his seminal work on the Devi's worship as stated earlier, and made a list of the Mahapeethas of Shakti worship, which brings under a single umbrella the various cultural narratives surrounding the Devi's sect. As an artist, devotee, poet and bhakt, he is honoured at the Sharada Devi Peetha.

The worship of the Devi in Maihar is similar to the customs which are followed at the Sharada temple in Sringeri in Karnataka, where it is believed that Sankaracharya first established her monastery or math. There are many tales of Sankaracharya crossing paths with the Devi herself, that is the Goddess Saraswati. He is said to have propagated his Sanatana Dharma with the blessings of the Devi. At her Peetha in Maihar, the devotees pay their respects to her sons Ganesha and Kartikeya besides her, and to Shiva in his Kaalbhairava form, a representation of mortal time. In addition, one can find the Goddess in her two most opposing forms at this Peetha, one as the warrior Kali and the other as the householder Gauri.

Today the Sharada Devi temple is represented by a committee that is run by the district collector. The original structure of the shrine is believed to have been built in the 6th century. In those days, animal sacrifice was conducted regularly up until the point when they were outlawed by the king of the region in the year 1922.

There is a lot of rich folkloric history attached to the temple. One of these tales talk of the brothers Alha and Udal, who were generals in the Chandela army of Bundelkhand back in the 12th century. There is a pond near the temple where they would regularly carry out physically vigorous exercises for their strength, and end the day with the worship of the Goddess. One day, they had to face King Prithviraj Chauhan in battle, wherein Udal was killed. Alha, ready to avenge his brother's death by taking Prithviraj's life, was stopped by Devi Sharada, who appeared before him. As a true devotee of the Goddess, Alha instead offered his own head to the Devi. Pleased by his devotion, she brought both the brothers back to life, forever protecting them. As per the local lore about the temple, the two generals still visit the temple as immortal beings and live out their time in the deep forests of the region.

In another tale from the region, once a cowherd brought his cows to the dense greenery of the Trikuta Hill. Here he discovered a golden cow amidst his own herd. Intrigued, he followed it to see where it went. His intention was to charge the owner for allowing the cow to graze in his territory, but the cow led the cowherd to a cave where an old lady sat offering him grains as her fee. When he returned home that evening, the grains had turned into jewels, which he took straight to the king. The king, now curious, decided to visit the old lady himself, for no one had heard of such a woman living deep in the forest. That night, Sharada Devi visited the king in his dreams, revealing to him that the old lady was none other than the Devi herself. She asked the King to build a shrine for her to rest in and a clear pathway for her devotees to find their way to her, and it was from this dream that the journey to the Sharada Devi Shakti Peetha begins.

37

Mangal Chandika Shakti Peetha
Ujjain, Madhya Pradesh

*Ujjayinyaam Kuurparan-Ca Maanggalya
Kapilaambarah
Bhairavah Siddhi-Dah Saakssaad-Devii
Manggalacannddikaa ||16||20*

[At Ujjayini, my auspicious kurpara, or elbow, fell. Kapilambara, whose name literally means he who is wearing red clothes, is the Bhairava there. The Devi Mangala Chandika, meaning the auspicious Chandika, lives there and visibly gives Siddhi or spiritual accomplishments, to all her devotees.]

Ujjain in Madhya Pradesh is one among the older cities of India. In ancient times it was a place of great significance for scholars who made their astronomical and geographical calculations from here. Interestingly, Ujjain holds great import geographically since the Tropic of Cancer passes through the city, where it is intersected by the Prime Meridian, much before Greenwich was discovered. Ujjain was mentioned in accounts of various visiting scholars including

---

[20]https://greenmesg.org/stotras/durga/shakti_peethas.php

Ptolemy of Greece who gave it the name 'Ozene'.

The name 'Ujjain' means the 'victorious city,' as it was known in ancient times. It is one of the seven sacred cities of India known in Hindi as Sapta Puri. In the Puranic texts it is mentioned in the episode of the churning of the ocean with Shiva, Vishnu, the devas and the asuras, for amrit, or the elixir of immortality. When the amrit finally emerged, the devas and asuras immediately started fighting among themselves for ownership. Amidst this tussle, some of the amrit fell on the ground; four drops of this fell at Ujjain, and till date, the devout who visit the city take a dip in the river Shipra that runs through the city to cleanse their souls. Every 12 years, the city plays host to the Kumbh Mela or Mahakumbha, a festival commemorating the utmost sanctity of the many streams of Hinduism.

As a pilgrim centre, the city is blessed with temples of various iconic deities, and all year round, one can find pilgrims visiting its star-like spread of shrines. The Devi temple here is known as Harsiddhi Mata and it can be recognized by its distinct red roof and spire. This is a celebrated Shakti Peetha, where it is believed that the Devi's elbow fell. The patron god of the city is Shiva, and the five-storied Mahakaleshwar temple with the sculpted shikhara is one of the 12 jyotirlingams, with this one being the most centrally located temple in the geography of the jyotirlingams. According to the mythos of Shiva jyotirlingams, he is believed to appear as a column of light at these 12 temple sites. In Puranic texts, there is a verse which elucidates the place of Ujjain in the context of the jyotirlingams, where Shiva is seen as presiding over the three worlds—he is Taralinga in the skies, Hatkeshwara beneath the ground, and Mahakal on Earth, that is Mrityulok, where mortals exist.[21]

In the Shakta tradition, the Devi remains close to her consort, who, in Ujjain, is close at hand to the jyotirlingams.

---

[21]Eck, D.L. (2012). *India: A Sacred Geography*. Harmony.

Her devotees, who come visiting her here, worship her as Annapurna, the Mother Goddess, who sustains and feeds all of creation. Here she is depicted in a dark, vermilion-tinged sculpture which stands between her trinity forms, Mahalakshmi and Mahasaraswati. In Ujjain, one finds many overlapping and intersecting aspects of the Devi. According to Sankaracharya's *Shakti Stotram,* the Devi here is Mahakali. In Puranic literature, she is described as part of the celestial trinity that assumes both masculine and feminine forms. Stemming from this tri-fold aspect of the Devi's power, one finds a Sri Yantra in the garbhagriha or the innermost sanctum of the temple. The tantric ritual diagram is a representation of the Tripura Sundari, an aspect of the Devi which personifies her triadic powers.

Devi Mahakali is the same as Mahakal, a manifestation of divine time, and the consort of Shiva who presides over the city, the god of destruction who swallows the cosmic whole. Mahakali is thus the Mahadevi, the Shakti without whom Mahakal cannot exist. At the temple of Harsiddhi, the Goddess is also worshiped as Annapurna, for it is she who ensures that there is an abundance of food for existence to continue to sustain itself. She is the mother in the sphere of the home, the Goddess of the kitchen whose prime function is to stave off hunger, and as an extension to her, Shiva then becomes Pashupati or the Lord of all Creatures.

In *Tantra Chudamani,* there is a verse regarding the Goddess Mangala Chandika which describes her as the principal Devi form at the Ujjain Shakti Peetha. Perhaps stemming from this, was born the local lore that narrates an episode where Shiva called upon the Devi to fight against the demons, Chanda and Munda, who were wreaking havoc upon the three lokas. When she slayed the demons, she did so in her Chandi form, and on watching the Devi's display of strength and divinity, Shiva was so pleased that he gave her a special name, which was Harsiddhi, the one who conquers all.

At the entrance to the Harsiddhi temple, the garbhagriha faces the east, where one finds two tall, traditional lamp posts. These are a part of a glittering display of lit diyas which bring the place to life in the hours of dusk. This is an especially magnificent sight during the Navratri festival and was introduced by the Marathas who renovated the temple in the 18th century.

38

Lalita Devi Shakti Peetha
Prayagraj, Uttar Pradesh

Anggulii-Vrindam Hastasya Prayaage Lalitaa Bhavah|[22]

[The anguli vrinda, or group of fingers of my hand, fell at Prayagraj. There the Devi is known as Lalita, whose name literally means one who is playful and the Bhairava is called Bhavah, whose name literally means the essence of existence.]

It is here in the town of Misrikh Neemsar on the banks of the river Gomti that we find Naimisharanya, the site of a rich mythos that goes far back into antiquity. At a distance of 100 km from Prayag, which is the holy confluence of the rivers Ganga and Yamuna, Naimisharanya is known as the land where sages and yogis frequently carried out rigorous meditations and tapas, creating a number of Puranic texts under leafy banyan trees. It is believed that even Veda Vyas organized Vedic literature into the four vedas in the forests surrounding the town. This is the also region that inspired the epic poems, the Ramayana and the Mahabharata, with many episodes taking place in this area. Naturally, this makes Naimisharanya a significant place for the devout, and as such, it has its own sacred geography of temples

---

[22]https://greenmesg.org/stotras/durga/shakti_peethas.php

in and around the town, most prominent among which is the Lalita Devi Shakti Peetha.

According to *Tantra Chudamani*, a text devoted to the Devi, this was the place where Devi Sati's fingers fell. This fact is often contested, with some believing that this was where the Devi's heart fell instead. Nonetheless, this site is of much significance to Shakti worship, and the Goddess is adored here in her many aspects, primarily as Lalita and Madhaveshwari. The shrine of Lalita Devi shows her with a lion at her feet, widely recognized as a representation of her vehicle or vahan. A number of legends surround the town of Naimisharanya, one of which recalls a time when the three gods, Brahma, Vishnu and Mahesh, made a joint appearance, energizing the place with their spiritual energy. It is believed thus that observing penance here helps one attain their place in Brahmaloka, a plane of existence which is parallel to attaining moksha.

The name 'Lalita' means a vision of ultimate beauty and as such, the Devi is also Rajarajeshwari or the queen of kings. Her depiction signifies her power as she is also the Tripura Sundari, the supreme Devi, in the three worlds, the source of the triadic power that fuels all existence. Her ten fingernails are representational of Lord Vishnu's ten avataras and in that respect, she is also closely associated with him as the source of his Shakti.

In another tale of the deity, Brahma calls upon Lalita Devi to annihilate demons, and the Goddess, as a protective force in the cosmos, chooses to destroy all the ills of the world. Her identity as Lalita Devi in particular is all-encompassing of this primordial energy. She is also perceived as Shiva's consort, identified as a Mahavidya, one of the ten wisdoms of Adi Shakti. The Devi's multidimensional persona is unpacked in the elaborate text of *Lalit Sahasranama*, a hymn recalling the thousand names of Lalita Devi. David Kinsley's *Tantric Visions of the Divine Feminine* describes Lalita as 'identical with certain philosophical attributes such as the Brahman'. Her form is both benevolent and frightening and as prakriti, she is composed of atman, shakti and purusha. Her temple in Prayag has a cantilever entrance frame which is adorned with sculptures of elephants representational of royalty and magnificence. Not too far from the Devi's shrine is a small circular pond, Chakrakund ('chakra' meaning 'wheel' and 'kund' meaning 'pond'), and along it, a row of shrines of minor deities.

From this pond comes an alternative story which first makes an appearance in the *Vayu Purana*. When the sages on Earth were looking for a place to go into samadhi unperturbed, they reached out to Brahma for relief from the Age of Kali, a vedic epoch when chaos ran rampant across the world. Brahma rolled out his celestial wheel and asked them to follow it, saying that they would find the place they so desired at the site where the wheel breaks. It was at Chakrakund that the wheel finally broke and created a fissure, causing water to gush out with great ferocity. Eventually Devi Lalita had to intervene, fixing the wheel and containing the flow, and the pond was thus formed. The Chakrakund makes another appearance in the epic poem Mahabharata, as the place where the Pandavas had built a secret tunnel during their exile as a way to escape and wage war against their cousins, the Kauravas.

Her devotees hold her to the greatest esteem, and hymns that praise her talk of her ability to take one through the illusion of life towards the light of knowledge and enlightenment.

Sri manthra raja sadruso yadha manthro vidhyate
Devatha Lalita thulyaa yadhaa nashti ghatodhbhava

[There are no chants which equal the Sri Mantra Raja Agastya! There is no Goddess equivalent to Lalita...]
—LALITA SAHASRANAMA

39

Devagarbha Shakti Peetha
Kanchipuram, Tamil Nadu

*Kaancii-Desho Ca Kangkaalo Bhairavo Ruru-Naamakah |
Devataa Devagarbha-[A]akhyaa Nitambah
Kaalamaadhave ||34||23*

[At Kanchi, my kankaala or skeleton fell. There the Bhairava has the name Ruru. The Devata, implying here the Devi, is named Devagarbha, whose name literally means the womb of divinity.]

Along the breezy east coast of Tamil Nadu we have Kanchipuram, a region known not only for its beautiful handwoven saris, but also for its rich multitudes of philosophical traditions and their diverse religious activities. Interestingly, the hand-weaving traditions and the religious philosophies inspire and mutually benefit from one another. The magnificent temples are known to be architectural wonders constructed under royal and aristocratic patronage.

In the town of Kanchipuram, beside the river Polar, we have the Kamakshi Amman temple, which was built during the rule of the Pallava dynasty. This is a Shakti Peetha, where Sati's backbone or, as some claim, her nabhi, or midriff, fell. This is

---

[23]https://greenmesg.org/stotras/durga/shakti_peethas.php

why it is also called Nabisthana Ottiyana Peetam. This is another one of the Mahapeethas that were listed under Sankaracharya's 18 holy sites for the Devi's worship. According to folklore, he himself consecrated the temple and it was the Pandaya who established the innermost sanctum or the garbhagriha in the 14th century, prior to the recent renovations.

Kanchipuram has the unique honour of being one of the Mokshapuris in Indian mythology. These are a group of sites which offer salvation, also known colloquially as Sapta Puri. In the pilgrim circuit it is recognized as a city of 100 temples. In Puranic texts there is a beautiful significance associated with Kanchipuram, which, along with Kashi, is considered to be the eyes of Lord Shiva. The town itself has 108 Shiva temples, and the Kamakshi Amman temple is the only shrine where the Devi is worshipped independently of her divine consort.

Inside the temple there is an intricately carved spire that stands tall above the garbhagriha, which is decorated with gold highlights. Within it, one is greeted with a cross-legged Kamakshi Devi in padmasana; in her four hands she holds a sugarcane stem; a pushpabana, or flower arrow; a pasa, or knotted rope; and an angusa, or goad. It was believed that the Devi meditated in this spot on the tip of a needle while she was surrounded by the five flaming pits of fire also known as the panchagni, in order for her to be able to transcend all worldly desires.

Devi Kamakshi is known as a powerful force of creation and in the town of Kanchipuram, she is viewed as closely associated with Devi Mahalakshmi or in some combination of Shakti and Lakshmi. Some even believe her to be linked to Saraswati as the Goddess, bestowing spiritual knowledge and wisdom and as such, Kamakshi then becomes the Devi who represents both Saraswati and Lakshmi with her two eyes, and Shakti with her being.

To the north of the temple is a beautiful sculpture of the Devi represented as Mahishasuramardini. In this powerful warrior

Kamakshi Amman Temple
Photo: Creative Commons/SINHA

form, she is the epitome of feminine energy, both creative and destructive, balancing the union of the cosmos. The Kamakshi Amman temple is the embodiment of all of these qualities of the Devi, ascribed to her as the primordial tri-fold force—Durga, Lakshmi and Saraswati. She is much like the all-encompassing Lalit Tripura Sundari, dazzling across the three lokas.

> *sindūrāruṇa vigrahāṁ trinayanāṁ māṇikyamauli sphurat*
> *tārā nāyaka śekharāṁ smitamukhī māpīna vakṣoruhām |*
> *pāṇibhyāmalipūrṇa ratna caṣakaṁ raktotpalaṁ bibhratīṁ*
> *saumyāṁ ratna ghaṭastha raktacaraṇāṁ*
> *dhyāyet parāmambikām ||*

[Let us meditate on the Divine Mother whose body has the red hue of vermilion, who has three eyes, who wears a beautiful crown studded with rubies, who is adorned with the crescent Moon, whose face sports a beautiful smile indicating compassion, who has beautiful limbs, and whose one hand holds a jewel-studded golden vessel filled with nectar, while the other, a red lotus flower.]

—LALITA SAHASRANAMA STOTRAM[24]

Devi Kamakshi is the bestower of miraculous boons, making even the mute speak words of great beauty. According to the *Markandeya Purana*, Raja Dashratha visited the town to pray to the Goddess for a child. To this day, this practice is prevalent and couples from all over the country come to the shrine of the Devi with the hopes of leaving with her prasada and blessings for a child.

---

[24]https://www.manblunder.com/articlesview/sri-lalita-sahasranama-stotram

40

Guhyeshwari Shakti Peetha
Kathmandu, Nepal

*Om asya śrīguhyakālīsahasranāmastotrasya
śrītripuraghna ṛṣiḥ |
anuṣṭup chandaḥ | ekavaktrādiśatavaktrāntā śrīguhyakālīdevatā |
phrūṃ bījaṃ | khraiṃ khraiṃ
śaktiḥ | chrīṃ khrīṃ kīlakaṃ |
puruṣārthacatuṣṭayasādhanapūrvakaśrī
caṇḍayogeśvarīprītyarthe
jape viniyogaḥ |Oṃ̇ tatsat|*

—SRI GUHYAKALI SAHASRANAMA STOTRAM[25]

Running through Nepal's capital city Kathmandu, in the lower Himalayas, is River Bagmati, which flows southwards to meet the Ganga in the state of Bihar. Despite being a commercial centre, Bagmati, much like Ganga, holds great spiritual significance. Each evening, devotees come to her banks, and wait opposite the twin temples of Guhyakali and Pashupatinath, for the evening aarti, a magnificent scene to bear witness to.

---

[25]https://sanskritdocuments.org/doc_devi/guhyakAlIsahasran Amastotram. html?lang=iast

The site of these two temples is revered as a Shakti Peetha, and according to legend, it is here that Devi Sati's knee fell. In an alternative belief, the prefix 'Guhya' roughly translates to 'hidden' in the esoteric sense, and it is sometimes believed that this is the spot where the Devi's reproductive organ fell, marking the temple with special significance.

In Kathmandu, the Devi's worship has been a norm from ancient times: their Kumari tradition bears witness to this. Such an observance was a significant part of royal rituals and customs in the 18th century when the Kumari tradition first began—of a young girl being chosen as the living Goddess of Nepal with whose blessings the kingdom would thrive. The Devi at the Guhyeshwari temple is an amalgamation of various concurrent religious philosophies. The Goddess is worshipped in her Vajrayogini form from Mahayana Buddhism and tantric worship. In tantric practices, it is believed that one attains enlightenment through various sadhanas which are the mainstay in this form of worship done before Goddess Vajrayogini. The cult of the tantric Goddess Vajrayogini flowered in India between the 10th and 12th centuries CE at a mature phase of Buddhism.[26] The Buddhists of the Vajrayana sect of the Newari community were considered the original inhabitants of the Kathmandu Valley, and known for their worship of the Goddess, presenting her with the traditional Newari Bhog as part of the rituals of prayer.

Vajrayogini Devi is often associated with the bloodthirsty Chhinnamasta Devi, the warrior goddess, who beheads herself to feed and nourish those who accompanied her in battle and is one of the Devi's Dus Mahavidyas, or knowledge streams. Similarly in the Buddhist traditions, Goddess Vajrayogini is herself considered the enlightened one, or the Buddha. In Puranic texts, the Mahavidyas are, at times, represented alongside a group

---

[26]English, E. (2013). *Vajrayogini: Her Visualization, Rituals, and Forms*. Simon and Schuster.

of thousand 'Guhyakalis,' or minor goddesses who emerge from the Devi and are helpful in ascribing the ultimate reality and creation from the Mahavidyas. They emerge from the Devi as Sati, Kali, Durga or Parvati. It is believed there are ten female counterparts of the ten avataras of Vishnu; however, sometimes their association is stronger with Shiva due to the Dus Mahavidya episode from the *Shiva Purana*. It is indeed noticeable in the Guhyeshwari temple that the two shrines of the Devi and Pashupati stand right beside one another, built no more than a kilometre apart. This is in line with the Shiva and Shakta worship, according to which the Devi always comes before her consort.

Guhyeshwari Shakti Peetha is also considered to be the place of the hidden Kali or the Guhyakali. According to tantric literature, the Goddess is associated with serpents, worshipped with wine and is an aspect of Kali herself.[27] It is these fierce identifiers of the Divine Mother Goddess, at the Devi's shrine depicting the cycles of birth and death, which have been a guiding principle for Bagmati's ghats where funeral pyres are found burning every day. People come from all over Nepal to cremate their loved ones at these ghats where they are believed to find salvation. Since Kali is, in one form or another, the primary deity of the temple and Goddess of the cremation ground, a skeleton's image decorates the entrance of the temple. It is as an extension of her form that at this temple, Shiva is also worshipped as Kapali, or the bearer of skulls. Inside the temple, the Devi's shrine greets its devotees with a heavy scent of incense and marigolds as visitors bow before the image of Devi Guhyakali, partaking in her darshan. The garbhagriha has a metallic doorframe with rich imagery featuring the various forms of the Devi carved intricately. Beside it is the Bhairava Kund, a holy spot named after the Devi's divine consort and eternal companion.

---

[27]Kinsley, D. (1998). *Tantric visions of the Divine Feminine*. Delhi: Motilal.

During the 17th century, King Pratap Malla of Kathmandu, a committed patron of the arts, had the temple built according to the Buddhist style, with a pagoda-like roof. It is here that we also have the Pashupatinath shrine, dedicated to Shiva as the Lord of Animals. It is not too far away from the Devi's. The Pashupatinath shrine predates the Devi's shrine, and it is believed that the priests of the temple can accurately predict one's time of death. During the ten days and nine nights of the Navratras—called Dashain in Nepal—the footfall at the Guhyeshwari temple increases manyfold. As hundreds come to offer prayers and celebrate the Goddess who is victorious over evil, the shrine is surrounded by special sculptures depicting her many martial forms.

41

Narmada Shakti Peetha
Amarkantak, Madhya Pradesh

Punar-Bhava-Abdhi-Janma-Jam
Bhava-Abdhi-Duhkha-Varmade
Tvadiiya-Paada-Pangkajam
Namaami Devi Narmade ||4||

[Your water, which is a protective shield against the sorrows of the ocean of worldly existence, caused by repeated births in this ocean of samsara (worldly existence), O Devi Narmada, I bow down to your lotus feet, please give me your refuge.]

—NARMADA ASHTAKAM[28]

In the mountainous region of Madhya Pradesh is a deep green landscape of forested woods which are marked by the Satpura, Vindhya and Maikal ranges, formed millions of years ago. Beside their terrain is the robust flow of River Narmada and Son's clear waters, having risen out of the Maikal hills at the majestic site and pilgrim town of Amarkantak respectively.

The Narmada belongs to a network of seven sacred rivers, which include the Himalayan river network of Ganga, Yamuna

---

[28]https://greenmesg.org/stotras/narmada/narmadashtakam.php

Narmada Kund Temple
Photo: Creative Commons/Kailash Mohankar

Kaveri and Sindhu, Godavari from the Western Ghats, and the mythical Saraswati, believed to have dried up over the ages. It is a well-established belief among the devout that if one is touched by the waters of any one of these seven sacred rivers, they are purified for this life and those to come. The Narmada has a special place among these rivers because many say that to even catch a glimpse of the Narmada is enough to attain moksha or enlightenment. There is a quaint little tale in the Puranic texts, namely the *Shiva Purana,* which describes how at least once a year, the river Ganga, which takes on all the sins and ills of mankind upon herself, finds herself dirty and needs a cleansing. It is at this time that she transforms herself into a black cow, meeting the waters of the Narmada to purify herself.[29]

As the Narmada flows down from the hills, it is given the name of Rewa. In the *Rewa Mahatamya* from the *Skanda Purana,* we learn that the hills of the region of Madhya Pradesh are older than even the Himalayas. In the Puranic texts, the Narmada is an emblem of immortality. The source of the river lies in one of India's most prominent spiritual sites as the 'king of pilgrimages'. Thousands of devotees come to undertake the processional circumambulation of the river, known as Narmada Parikrama. Sadly, because of the recent urbanization and the hike in developmental projects, the practice of the parikrama is slowly and steadily dwindling.

In *Tantra Chudamani*, we are told that the Devi's hips were found at a site near the Narmada. This is the site of the Narmada Shakti Peetha. The Devi here is Shona or Sona and her Bhairava is called Bhadrasena. Alternatively, many believe that the Devi's hips fell at a place called Kalmadhav and here she is worshipped in her more fearsome forms of Kali and Asitang. Both of these sites can be traced back to the town of Amarkantak—the first is

---

[29]Warrier, S. (2014). *Kamandalu: The Seven Sacred Rivers of Hinduism.* Mayur University.

the source of the Narmada or Narmada Udgam, and the second is the origin of the river Son at Sonmuda, a short distance of 2 km from the former. The rivers have a beautiful topography and they flow in the opposite directions to each other. It is believed in Indic mythology that they are representational of two tears streaming down Brahma the Creator's face.

The temple structures of Narmada Udgam are attributed to the rule of the Kaluchuris from the 11th century. White temples decked with red flags dot the landscape of Narmada Udgam. Goddess Narmada's innermost sanctum is among a group of shrines in a kund or pond which is made up of the waters from the Narmada. Visitors can pay obeisance here. However, they are not allowed to step within its waters. Pilgrims visiting the Peetha bow before the black stone of the Narmada Devi idol; an offering of coconuts and batasa sweets are also made to her.

The Devi at Amarkantak is in the image of a river goddess, which evolved from the various myths surrounding the holy status of the river Narmada. There is a tale that one day, Lord Shiva sat deep in meditation on a mountain top. The sweat that gathered on his brow from the strain of concentration flowed down as the Narmada.[30] This story's origin is much like that of the origin of the river Ganga, and it is here that their association with Adi Shakti comes from, as a source of sustenance and purification. The temple complex at the Narmada Shakti Peetha has many icons of Parvati seated beside Lord Shiva, who is the Narmadeshwar lingam submerged in the kund.

The elliptical stones collected from the Narmada are found in various sites of worship all around the country. They are know as banalingam and are revered as the manifestation of Shiva himself. When mankind was overtaken by sins, Vishnu turned to Shiva, who took a drop of amrit, or the elixir of immortality, from the moon decked in his hair, which turned into a beautiful blue river

---

[30]Eck, D. L. (2012). *India: A Sacred Geography*. Harmony.

goddess. He asked her to flow through Earth in order to free its inhabitants of sin, assuring her that her waters will be filled with stones which will allow people to fulfil their aspirations.[31] A contemporary custom at Narmada Udgam is to determine the burden of one sins—if one is able to crouch and pass through with ease from underneath the black elephant sculpture in the complex, then they are considered to be pure of heart.

---

[31]Eck, D.L. (2012). India: *A Sacred Geography*. Harmony.

42

Bargabhima Devi Shakti Peetha

East Midnapore, West Bengal

*aruṇāṁ karuṇā taraṅgitākṣīṁ
dhṛta pāśāṅkuśa puṣpa bāṇacāpām |
aṇimādibhi rāvṛtāṁ mayūkhai-
rahamityeva vibhāvaye bhavānīm ||*

[I meditate on Bhavānī, the supreme happiness, whose colour is like the sun at dawn i.e. red in colour and from whom, rays of light are emanating. The compassion for her devotees comes out of her eyes like waves of the ocean. I meditate on her form called Bhavānī, a state of supreme happiness with beams of light].

—LALITA SAHASRANAMA STOTRAM[32]

The Rupnarayan, a tributary of the Hooghly, flows through East Midnapore or Purba Medinipur district of West Bengal. It is famed across all of Bengal for providing the coveted Hilsa fish. It is along the fertile banks of this tributary that the Bargabhima temple is situated at the famous Vibhash Shakti Peetha of Tamluk, or as it is locally known, Tamralipta. The village is a popular destination and pilgrim spot for the

---

[32]https://www.manblunder.com/articlesview/sri-lalita-sahasranama-stotram

devout. According to myths, this is where Devi Sati's ankles fell and the Goddess is known here as Bargabhima, Bhimarupa or Bhimakali. Each of these aspects is closely related to Devi Kali or Kapalini, and as such the main idol of worship is that of Kali, evoking her legendary stature as a warrior goddess, going into battle with demons. She embodies the warrior soul as she wields her trident and khadaga or sword, holding a severed head in her hand. The black lingam that is close at hand is her Bhairava, Sarvanand, he who bestows eternal pleasure, and is seen as accompanying the sculpture of the Goddess within her white marble temple complex.

In the state of Odisha, the Devi is worshipped as Kapalini and the demon-slayer Chamundi, whereby she stands as an integral deity in the Shaivite sect and worship. As Kapalini, she is literally associated with the kapala or skull. The temple of Barghabhima was built under the Mayur-Dhwaj dynasty for whom she was the kuldevi, or family deity. Thus the architecture of the temple is similar to an Oriya architectural aesthetic and has the typical double-roofed atchala style of Bengal.

In the tantric scriptures, Kali is shown in her frightening aspect as a dark-skinned, naked Goddess with large breasts, who is emaciated. She holds a sword and a severed head, and is standing victoriously on a corpse—assumed to be of her divine consort Lord Shiva—wearing a garland of freshly cut heads and a girdle of human hands. The corpses of children make up her ear ornaments. She is of the utmost importance among the Dus Mahavidyas—the first of the ten goddesses to make an appearance in the Shakta ideology. She has primary stature and is believed to make an appearance whenever Devi Sati or Devi Parvati are truly angered by the injustices of the mortal world. She is an enraged Parvati in the domestic sphere and a Durga on the battlefield. Here in the Shakti Peetha however, she is seen as a patron of thieves, and she has to be checked by Shiva in order to maintain balance on Earth.

Bargabhima Temple
Photo: Creative Commons/Arnab Dutta

According to a seminal work on Kali called *Encountering Kali: In the Margins, at the Centre, in the West*,[33] the imagery and worship of the Goddess went through an evolution through the ages in the eastern tradition of India, owing to it being the dominant culture of the region. When one explores the tantric tradition versus the Brahmanical tradition, the depictions and tales associated with her bring out the difference between the violent but independent nature of Kali versus the benevolent and domesticated consort of Shiva, which subverts the patriarchal dynamics in terms of the seat of power.

---

[33]McDermott, Rachel Fell, Jeffrey J. Kripal & Vira I. Heinz. (2003). *Encountering Kali*. University of California Press.

43

Bhadrakali Shakti Peetha
Kurukshetra, Haryana

*Kanyaashrame Ca Prssttham Me Nimisso Bhairavas-Tathaa |
Sarvaannii Devataa Tatra Kurukssetre Ca Gulphatah|*[34]

[At Kanyashrama, my pristha, or back, fell, and the Bhairava there is called Nimisha, whose name literally means 'a moment of time'. The Devata (implying Devi) there is known as Sarvani whose name literally means 'the wife of Shiva'. At Kurukshetra, my gulpha, or ankle, fell and there the Bhairava is called Sthanu, whose name literally means 'the one who is still' and the Devata (implying the Devi) is known as Savitri, whose name literally means 'the energiser'.]

The ancient town of Kurukshetra in Haryana is a site which is known for being a conglomerate of archeological excavations bearing the history of a millennia. Kurukshetra is given primacy in the *Matsya Purana* and in Panini's *Ashtadyayi,* written sometime between the 6th and 5th centuries BCE. It is also the place where the battle of Mahabharata was believed to have been fought, making it an epicentre for the devout. The stories attached to the town have

---
[34]https://greenmesg.org/stotras/durga/shakti_peethas.php

given birth to various temples and a rich iconography, with Kurukshetra becoming a centre for even Sikh pilgrims.

At a short distance from the popular pilgrimage site stands the Brahma Sarovar, near which the Devikoop Bhadrakali shrine is believed to be a Shakti Peetha. There are many stories associated with this temple, which is also known as the Savitri Peetha or the Kalika Peetha, for this is the spot where, if legend is to be believed, Devi Sati's ankle fell in a well, or koop. In the temple in Thanesar, the idol of worship is that of Bhadrakali. There is a marble sculpture which shows the Devi's bejewelled ankle atop a lotus. Devi Bhadrakali is dressed in golden jewels, with a protruding tongue. Sometimes the deity is shown holding a khadaga, and at other times, a trident. Three times a day, the aarti is offered to the Goddess and as in all Shakti Peethas, the idol of her consort Shiva is worshipped not too far off, in the form of Sthanu Shiva.

In the Puranic texts, Devi Bhadrakali is a fierce warrior who defeats Mahishasura and in these stories, she is closely associated with Durga. She is also Devi Mahamaya, or the one who has created the grand illusion of the mortal world. She is always depicted with 16 arms, three blazing red eyes and three crowns decking her heads. She wears a snake around her neck and glittering jewels hang from her lobes. She holds a thunderbolt, a lance, an axe and a mace, among many weapons of war. She also has a conch shell, a bell and a book, implying her ability to break past the illusions of the mortal world. Bhadrakali also holds a special place among the Dus Mahavidyas as a fearsome Goddess whose alternative is the beautiful Kamala, associated in many strains as Devi Lakshmi herself.

In the tantric tradition, especially in eastern India, Devi Bhadrakali is a form of the grim Kali, but she is also identified with the tantric Goddess Tara. In the folk traditions of the South, especially Kerala, Bhadrakali exists as a prime deity and important warrior created by Shiva to vanquish the demon

Darika, when Bhagvati, another name for Mahamaya, protects him. In her anger, she transforms into the frightening and violent Bhadrakali.

> *Jayanti Mangala Kali, Bhadrakali Kapalini*
> *Durga Kshama Shiva Dhatri Swaha Swadha Namostute Te* ||

[Salutations to Jayanti (who is ever victorious), Mangala (who is the bestower of auspiciousness), Kali (who is beyond kala or time), Bhadrakali (who is the controller of life and death, being beyond kala or time), Kapalini (who wears a garland of skulls). Salutations to Durga (who is durgati-nashini), Shivaa (who is ever auspicious and one with Shiva as his consort), Kshama (who is an embodiment of forbearance), Dhatri (who is the supporter of all beings), Swaha (who is the final receiver of the sacrificial oblations to gods) and Swadha (who is the final receiver of the sacrificial oblations to Manes); salutations to you.]

—DEVI MAHATAMYA[35]

The name 'Thanesar' is derived from Sthaneshwar, because the great lord of time and existence, Shiva, is worshipped here as Sthanu. This is the site where the central battle in the epic poem, Mahabharata, took place between the warrior princes, the Pandavas and their cousins, the Kauravas. As per the local lore, it was here that the Pandavas along with Sri Krishna, their teacher and guide, worshipped the Devi in her Bhadrakali temple before heading out to war. Once they were victorious, the Pandavas returned to the Devi's shrine and offered up their horses to the Goddess. Today, this tradition has evolved into an offering of silver, wood and clay horse figurines. There is another folk legend pertaining to the Bhadrakali Shakti Peetha, according

---

[35] https://greenmesg.org/stotras/durga/argala_stotram.php

to which, Krishna and his stepbrother Balaram had their first ritual haircut, or mundan, in this very temple. Since then, the practice of young children having their first mundans in the Devi's shrine has been followed.

In contemporary times, every Saturday, a langar or bhandar is organized for visiting pilgrims and during the Navratras in the Chaitra month, this practice is continued for an entire 15 days. There is also a Shobhayatra, a procession of devotees bearing red flags, which takes place in the temple.

44

Tripura Sundari Shakti Peetha
Udaipur, Tripura

Tripuraayaam Dakssa-Paado Devii Tripurasundarii |
Bhairavas-Tripureshan-Ca Sarva-Abhiisstta-Pradaayakah[36]

[At Tripura, my daksha pada, or right foot, fell, and the Devi there is known as Tripura Sundari, whose name literally means 'one whose beauty pervades the three divisions'.
The Bhairava there is called Tripuresh, whose name literally means 'the lord of the three divisions'.
The Devi here grants all wishes of the devotees.]

In the town of Udaipur, in the state of Tripura, perched atop a hill that stands beside the Kalyansagar lake, is a temple dedicated to Tripura Sundari, who is worshipped here as Kali. The temple site precedes the lake by almost 100 years. The hillock beside the lake is named Kuma, or tortoise, because the mound resembles a tortoise. The site is a Shakti Peetha and as legend has it, this is where the Devi's right foot fell. She is worshipped here beside her Bhairava, an aspect of her divine consort Lord Shiva, as Tripuresh, the lord of the three divisions or three worlds.

---

[36] https://greenmesg.org/stotras/durga/shakti_peethas.php

Tripura Sundari Temple
Photo: Creative Commons/Soman

It was somewhere between the late 15th and early 16th centuries, when Tripura was under the rule of Dhanya Manikya, known as a just and capable ruler with many conquests under his belt. He was a product of a dynasty that, in mythical lore, could trace their origins back to Yayati, a royal ancestor to the warring clans of Mahabharata. The dynasty that is believed to have come from the Bodo community of the Kirat people had migrated to the north-eastern parts of the subcontinent from the Himalayas, and established their rule in the state of Tripura.

Much like his ancestors and his father Dharma Manikya, Dhanya worshipped the Devi as their kuldevi or family deity. As was the practice in the Devi's worship, especially among the tribal or warrior kshatriya tribes, a large part of this ritual included human sacrifice, which would not exceed three times a year for the sake of balance. It was Dharma Manikya and his son Dhanya Manikya who were credited with building the Tripura Sundari temple in the capital of the state, Rangamanti, which was later renamed Udaipur after their descendant Udai Manikya.[37]

If legends are to be believed, Dhanya Manikya had obtained great strength and Siddhi from following the eight-fold yoga path called Ashtasiddhi. As a result of that, the Devi as Tripura Sundari appeared before him in his dream, asking him to transfer her stone idol from Chattol (modern day Chittagong or Chattogram in Bangladesh) to his kingdom. She did, however, place a condition on the king that wherever the idol would reach at the time of dawn is where it will eventually be consecrated. The deity was thus placed on the Kurma hillock and her temple there also goes by the name of Matabri, or 'the mother's house'.[38]

Uniquely for this region, one finds an interesting co-mingling of the Shaivite and Vaishnavite forms of worship through the

---

[37]Saigal, O. (1978). *Tripura*. Concept Publishing Company.
[38]Bera, G.K. (2010). *The Land of Fourteen Gods: Ethno-cultural Profile of Tripura*. Mittal Publications.

Devi. Folklore explains this through a quaint story about Dhanya Manikya, who, through an exercise of clairaudience, had acquired the knowledge from Goddess Ambika about Narayana or Vishnu, creating a union of their spiritual energies. Tripura is thus recognized as a place where one can find the tri-shakti or the powers of Brahma, Vishnu and Maheshwara, through the worship of the Devi.

Alternatively, when one studies the *Lalita Sahasranama* dedicated to Devi Tripura Sundari, we find that Lord Vishnu's ten avataras all stemmed from the great Goddess, each one forming from her own physical aspect, that is her ten fingernails. In *Saundaryalahiri*, the male trinity derives its shakti from Tripura Sundari, who is thus the primordial energy, the power that brings the universe to life.

In the *Bhagvat Purana*, she is worshipped as Matabri. Tripura Sundari along with Kali are aspects or celestial forms of the Mahavidyas, the ten knowledge goddess forms who emerged from Devi Sati when she was angered by Shiva for not being able to attend her father Daksha's yagna.[39] However one can't ignore Tripura Sundari's place as a tantric Goddess of immense power and independence, who is worshipped here as the dark and terrifying Kali. The main idol of the Devi in the Tripura Shakti Peetha is in the form of Kali or Tripureshwari. She is depicted in the form of a reddish-black stone idol. She holds in her four hands weapons of war, wearing a golden crown as she stands over Shiva. She is also referred to as Soroshi, and beside her main idol is a smaller idol lovingly addressed as 'Choti Maa', or the 'younger mother' who is Devi Soroshi herself. When the royal hunting parties would go out for leisure and pastimes, this idol would accompany them to ensure that they were always protected and blessed by the Goddess.

The temple structure is a tall, west-facing, 75-foot

---

[39] Sridhar, R. *Cult of the Goddess*.

building, and is painted entirely red. There are four walls with a rounded ceiling topped with a chaar-chala roof as per the local architectural aesthetic, which slants downward in four directions. It is similar to Bengali religious architecture. On the roof, there is a conical block, which is a stupa with alcoves. This resembles lotus blooms. Above that, in a bouquet-like structure, is the karanda, which holds the red jayodhha, or victory flag, ritualistic of the Devi.

The Devi is accordingly offered the first harvest of crops as is the tradition in most agriculturally led regions where she is worshipped, and given milk and anna bhog by the local communities. Earlier on, devotees would also sacrifice goats, pigeons, ducks and buffaloes to her; however, this practice has evolved into a token sacrifice of pumpkins and melons.

45

Kalika Shakti Peetha
Pavagadh, Gujarat

Tripuraayaam Dakssa-Paado Devii Tripurasundarii |
Bhairavas-Tripureshan.-Ca Sarva-Abhiisstta-Pradaayakah

[The Bhairava is called Nakuleesha at Kalipitha, where my daksha pada anguli, or the fingers of my right foot, fell. There the Devi gives all Siddhis or spiritual accomplishments, and there the Devata (implying Devi) is known as Kalika, whose name literally means 'the dark goddess'.]

Pavagadh in Gujarat is a short 50 km journey from the city of Vadodara. This arid prehistoric lava formation is believed to be the resting site of Devi Sati's pind, or where the fingers of her right foot fell. As such, the Devi is worshipped here as Kalika Mata. Many believe that the name of the site, 'Pavagadh', borrows from the word 'papa', or fire, owing to its origin story of being shaped by the fires of a volcano. The temple itself was built sometime between the late 10th and early 11th century, but because of this area's historic significance, it stays enclosed within the fortification of the Champaner-Pavagadh Archaeological Park, a UNESCO World Heritage Site.

At this Shakti Peetha, the Devi is worshipped in her fierce

Kalika Temple
Photo: Creative Commons/Arian Zwegers

Kali form, with traditional connotations towards a tribal goddess, worshipped primarily by the Bhil community. Beside her shrine is a neighbouring shrine dedicated to Lord Shiva in his Bhairava avatara as Lakulisa or Nakulisa, which dates from around the same period, made from the frightening ascetic fire of Shiva. In the 14th century, this area used to be under the control of a Rajput dynasty known as the Chauhans. In their religious philosophy, Devi Kali was worshipped as a principal deity. Interestingly enough, this is a deity who was widely favoured among the warrior class; as warriors themselves they would turn to her for blessings of victory in war. As such, she is represented in the temple even today as an idol with a red head called Mukhawto, representational of her victory.

The depiction of Kali in this Peetha has evolved from an ancient pre-agrarian deity to a feminine force of creation. As the Mother Goddess, she not only has the power to create but to take back what she has created, in a cycle of construction and destruction, maintaining an ever-shifting balance. She is also the terrifying demon-killing Goddess, more ferocious than the benevolent Parvati and even the battle-ready Durga.

The entire area around Pavagadh is populated by structures built over centuries by different ruling dynasties, making it an archaeological treasure trove. The ruins discovered in the area go back thousands of years to the Chalcolithic period, between the Stone and Copper Ages, adding a truly enriching and multifaceted history to the site.

The city shifted hands numerous times. In 1535, it was under the Mughal king, Humayun, when the capital shifted to Ahmedabad. One of the popular local legends of Pavagadh was that it was the birthplace of Baiju Bawra who features prominently in the stories of the famous 16th century musician Tansen as a rival. When the Mughals left, the area transferred hands to the Marathas for a short while, till it was finally taken over by the British in the 19th century. Through each reign, the Kalika Mata temple pilgrimage remained unobstructed and devotees would always make the trip to pay their obeisance as darshan to the Goddess.

Aside from the Shakti Peetha, the archaeological park also has a cluster of Jain temples decorated with intricate carvings, built between the 13th and 14th centuries. There are also some minor mosques such as the Jami Masjid from the Sultanate era, which shows a coming together of religious philosophies and faiths. One can find various stepwells and man-made lakes, stables and pavilions, in line with kingdoms that made their home in this town. There is a lot of overlapping architectural evidence of the multifaceted influence on this area, such as the Jain Kalpavriksha motif that can be found on the Shahi Masjid, and the Islamic-style dome on the Kalika Mata temple.

The Devi's shrine itself is approachable either on foot or via a ropeway. There is a story in the Puranas about the Rishi Vishwamitra, who was responsible for establishing the Devi's idol and consecrating the temple with her shakti. In fact, one of the three major rivers which originate from here is the Vishwamitri, named after him. There is in fact another story pertaining to the great sage which perhaps gives us an idea as to the origin of the name of Pavagadh. It is believed that he once prayed at the site of the hill before it came into being. Thus it was given to him as a gift by the gods when he requested that his cows should not fall into the deep valley that surrounds him. The hill that rises out of this valley is a quarter of the divine hill, hence Pavagadh. The Chaitra Navratri months during the nine-day and nine-night fasting period are considered to be the busiest time for the Devi's temple, with devotees swarming in to pay their respects to the great Goddess. At this time, a place of prime prominence is given to her mantras of Bahuchara, celebrating her place as the bestower of goodwill.

46

Vimala Devi Shakti Peetha
Puri, Odisha

*Bhuvaneshii Siddhi-Ruupaa Kiriitta-Sthaa Kiriittatah
Devataa Vimalaa Naamnii Samvartto Bhairavas-Tathaa*

[The Goddess of the Universe, who is in the form of Siddhi (i.e. one who grants spiritual accomplishments) abides in Kirita, where my Kirita (Diadem) had fallen.
The Devata (implying Devi) there is named Vimala (literally meaning one who is stainless and pure), and the Bhairava is Samvarta (literally meaning one who brings about the dissolution of creation)[40].]

Puri is one of the major pilgrim centres of the Indian subcontinent in the state of Odisha, where the shrines are scattered around the famed Lord Jagannath temple. In the southwest corner of this commercial-religious city is a shrine dedicated to the Devi as Vimala Devi, where she is worshipped alongside her Bhairava, Jagannath, the lord of the world. The temple architecture is built along the lines of a rekha deula, a gopuram-type pyramidical tower that rises above the main sanctum sanctorum. The Devi is revered here as Adi Shakti,

---

[40]https://greenmesg.org/stotras/durga/shakti_peethas.php

this being one of her four main Shakti Peethas as outlined in the Puranic texts. It is believed that this is where the Devi's pada khanda, or feet, fell and in recent years, this site has been recognized for its historic stature and placed under the care of the Archaeological Survey of India.

The idol of Goddess Vimala Devi is made of stone, with four hands, three of which hold a rosary, a mermaid sculpture and an amrit kalasa or goblet of the immortal elixir. Her fourth hand is in the Varada mudra, a gesture of blessing. In a recent study on the identity of Vimala Devi in the context of Shakti, she is seen as the feminine energy behind all the male devas or devotees, and is explored through the personified relationships with their individual shakti or the ephemeral.[41]

As the Mother Goddess Amba from Vedic texts, namely the *Yajurveda*, she is also known as Subhadrika and can be associated with Subhadra, the Devi who accompanies Jagannath in the main Jagannath shrine devoted to Sri Krishna in the central temple complex of Puri. According to the *Skanda Purana*, Subhadra was historically recognized as either Krishna's wife or his sister, as she appears in the Mahabharata. Uniquely at the Vimala Devi temple of Puri, it is compulsory to take the prasada that is offered to Jagannath, first to Vimala Devi and then to Lord Jagannath himself, reinstating the place of Devi worship in context to the trinity of godheads. It is only after the Devi's darshan that the prasada can be distributed to the devotees assembled at the Jagannath shrine as the Mahaprasad. Vimala Devi can further be interpreted in two aspects—one as a tribal Goddess to Odisha's tribal community and the second, similar to the tantric Goddess Vajrayana, who originates from the Buddhist tradition.

Most often we see her associated with Devi Vajrayana as the Vimala Peetha is considered to be a significant tantric Siddhapeetha. The Brahmin priests of the Jagannath temple are

---

[41]Tripathi, G.C. *Cult of the Goddess*.

in fact Shakta worshippers and as such, Devi Vimala is their ishtadeva, or deity. There is some contention regarding which part of the Devi exists in this Shakti Peetha, as according to the text of *Tantra Chudamani*, in Utkal, one of the ancient names of Odisha, it was Devi Sati's nabhi, or navel, that fell to the ground instead of her feet. However scholars have not been able to come to an agreement on this. In the *Matsya Purana* there is a mention of a Vimala Devi at Purushottam Kshetra, which in other places is known as Utkal or Odisha, and therefore we know that the aspect of Shakti which is worshipped here is most definitely Vimala Devi.

Puri has historically been a region dominated by a puritanical form of Brahminism founded on the worship of Shiva, Surya, and Krishna as Jagannath. As Kalinga from Ashoka's Mauryan Empire, this was also the land through which Brahminism, Buddhism and Jainism passed. Temples like the Jagannath temple were established at a time when Shaivite worship was ebbing and Vaishnavite worship was gaining royal patronage. Both the Vimala Devi Peetha and the Jagannath shrine were built in the early 12th century during the reign of King Codganga from the Shaivite Ganga clan.[42]

However, when we delve deep into Puranic texts, we see that both Shiva and Vishnu stem from the same power—a cosmic wholeness that is the Devi. In the *Devi Bhagvata Purana*, there is a conversation between Vishnu and his consort Lakshmi in which he explains that he meditates upon Shiva, and that Shiva meditates upon him, bound as they are by a powerful universal love that makes them one, even if they are separate. Therefore Shiva's Bhairava avatara here, as Vishnu, starts to make more sense and Vimala is thus as much Lakshmi as she is Uma-Parvati. In the Shakti Peetha however, Vimala is worshipped in her

---

[42]Starza, O.M. (1993). *The Jagannatha temple at Puri: Its Architecture, Art, and Cult* (Vol. 15). Brill.

Mahishasuramardini form.

Due to the wide presence of Buddhism in this region, many scholars regard Jagannath as Buddha, Vishnu's ninth incarnation. There is in fact even a mural in the complex which depicts the Buddha as one of Narayana's incarnations. Thus the connection of Vimala to the tantric texts, as Vajrayana, starts to emerge. However, to a large extent, Vimala Devi's significance comes from Sankaracharya, who was credited with building four important holy sites to the Devi in four cardinal directions. The great sage was believed to have established the worship of Vimala as Adi Shakti or Mahadevi at the site of the Jagannath temple, which together made this place a Govindapeetha.

During the Navratras in autumn, the Goddess used to be offered sacrificial goats which were shared with the priests. It was only in the 17th century that the mahaprasad became vegetarian under King Narsimha Dev, and animal sacrifices and meat offerings were banned as prasada.

47

Sugandha Devi Shakti Peetha
Shikarpur, Bangladesh

*Karaviire Tri-Netram Me Devii Mahissamardinii |
Krodhiisho Bhairavas-Tatra Sugandhaayaan-Ca
Naasikaa ||5||*

[At Sugandha, my naasika, or nose, fell. Here the Devi is Sugandha, whose name literally means 'pleasant fragrance', and the Bhairava there is Triambak whose name literally means 'the lord of the three worlds'.]

In the idyllic village of Shikarpur, north of Barisal in Bangladesh, is the temple dedicated to Goddess Sugandha. This shrine is one of the Shakti Peethas and here the Goddess is worshipped alongside her Bhairava, Triambak, the lord of the three worlds. The Ponabalia shrine itself is a short distance from the Devi's temple, falling in Shamrail village, situated on the banks of River Sunanda. It is believed that this was the place where Devi Sati's nose fell when Vishnu dismembered her physical corpse. According to the *Agama Shastra*, no temple shadow should ever fall upon the river, but in this spot one can see the temple shadow falling on the running water of the Sunanda, adding a spiritual energy and an auspiciousness to the waters of this great river.

While the origin of this temple or how far back it dates is not noted in any historical text, people believe it to be an ancient site simply on the basis of its structure and the aesthetic philosophy of the designs decorating this temple. The temple wall is peppered with carvings of Hindu gods and goddesses, with various sculptures on its stone walls depicting episodes from Puranic texts.

The Sugandha Shakti Peetha is known for its famed ritual of Shiva Chaturdashi, which falls on the fourteenth moon of the month of March when thousands of devotees swarm to the temple to worship the Lord as Triambak. If one wants to attend the procession, one has to come via the Jalkati station, from where one has to travel a short distance of 8 km to the temple. Devotees come with flags tied around their heads, carrying fruits and milk as offerings for the deities.

There is a special, ferocious energy that surrounds the worship of the Goddess. She is Shakti here—the basis of life itself—and as Shakti, she surpasses the feminine and the masculine despite being primarily associated with the Great Divine Goddess or Mahadevi. The Goddess is usually known for her supremacy over all living beings as the divine creator and yet, as is the case with every Shakti Peetha, she is worshipped alongside her consort or Bhairava form. It is interesting to note that the Devi's shakti is given direction through her relational union with her male counterpart, just the way the power or spiritual energy that the male devata wields comes from the Devi. In the mortal plane, neither can exist in the absence of the other, and yet in the primordial form and the esoteric plane, the Devi alone is all-encompassing.

At this point we think of Kali, a conundrum of a Goddess who charts a path between these two aspects of Adi Shakti, as both an independent goddess as well as a consort goddess. On one hand she is the supreme goddess who has unquestionable power over her domain, whether that is in a demanding maternal form or simply a container of immense, raw, uncontrollable natural force; on the other hand, it is her relationship with Shiva, her divine consort, which acts as a dam, as a source of balance to this unbridled force of creative and destructive power.

The Shakti Peetha thus is the place of union of these divergent roles of the Goddess, as both an independent deity and a goddess of the mortal world, which provides the devotee with a reference to life, a path to achieving spiritual enlightenment via the way of the world.

48

Tripurmalini Devi Shakti Peetha
Jalandhar, Punjab

Bhiissanno Bhairavastatra Devii Tripuramaalinii ||9||

[There at Jalandhar, the Bhairava is known as Bhishan whose name literally means 'the terrible' and the Devi is known as Tripurmalini whose name literally means 'garlanding the three worlds'.]

Devi Tripurmalini Dham is among the famous Shakti Peethas of North India. The temple is situated in Jalandhar in the state of Punjab. It is believed that this is the spot where Devi Sati's baam sthan, or left breast, fell. When Lord Shiva went to the various Shakti Peethas across the subcontinent to consecrate the shrines with the Devi's pind, it is believed that at Jalandhar—the site also known as Shri Omkareshwary—he rubbed his jattas, or long dreadlocks, in the soil, which was perfumed with the scent of sandalwood. He deputed Bhishan, his Bhairava form, to protect this place and after its establishment, took three parikramas of the sacred lake beside the shrine. The spot where his parikramas were completed is where a Shiva lingam was established. Many of the greatest sages of the ancient times were known to have complete rigorous sadhanas in this temple complex.

According to the folklore of the region, Sankaracharya the great sage from South India, on his visit to the Shakti Peetha, decreed that the pind revealed in the Dwapara Yuga[43] should always be covered since the Devi's left breast had fallen here. In order to keep the Goddess' modesty, he established a beautiful idol on top of it, which is said to have been discovered in the sacred lake beside the temple. There is a strong belief that those who worship the Devi here with a true heart have her personal audience and have their wishes realized in no time, or turant, giving her the colloquial moniker of 'Maa Turatpurni'.

The shrine of Tripurmalini Shakti Peetha has been renovated in recent years and new sections have been added to the temple. There is a pond, or talab, near the main temple which is a big attraction for visiting pilgrims and where the temple earned another name, Devi Talab temple. There is another temple not too far off, dedicated to Goddess Kali, and recently a structure resembling the Amarnath Cave temple was added to the complex.

As the Shakti Peetha where the Devi's left breast fell, the temple is also known as Sthanpeetha and the idol here bears the power associated with the tridevi—Mahasaraswati, Mahalakshmi and Mahakali. The Devi's tri-fold powers help fulfil all desires of her devotees. As is the practice in most Shakti Peethas, a diya or oil lamp is kept burning throughout the day and night and worshippers particularly visit the shrines on Tuesdays and Sundays, which are auspicious to the Devi.

There is a popular belief that those who die at Tripurmalini Shakti Peetha are ensured entrance into heaven on their passing. In fact, even the birds or animals who die at the Devi's feet here are granted freedom from the continuous cycle of life

---

[43]The third of the four yugas, where there are two pillars of religion—truthfulness and compassion.

and death. Another belief says that all the gods are present at this Shakti Peetha, awaiting an audience before the Mahadevi among her many earthly worshippers. Despite its great spiritual significance, it is one of the overlooked Shakti Peethas of the Devi and one can have a real adventure trying to find their way here.

Nonetheless, locally the temple is famed for its beauty and religious programming with various jagratas, or night-long prayer rituals, to the Devi and their mass jhankis, or dioramic representation of episodes from the Puranas. It is most popular in the months of the Navratras when pilgrims gather from far and wide to experience the Devi's darshan. Similarly during Ram Navami, there is a big celebration organized at the temple, celebrating the Rama avatara of Vishnu. North Indians have a robust culture of celebrating religious festivals and doing so in the form of big donations which often include gold. Through this practice, the temple has sustained itself well and can undertake constant maintenance and upgrades. In 2014, two gates beautifully decorated with wooden figurines were added. One can often find famous local folk singers and poets performing in the temple as part of their service, or sewa.

An integral part of the community, the Tripurmalini temple runs a goshala or cow shelter where hundreds of cow are kept, both those who provide milk and those that don't. The temple also runs a dharamshala and dispensary at a low cost to help those in need of its services.

49

Indrakshi Shakti Peetha
Manipallavam, Sri Lanka

*Langkaayaam Nuupuran-Cai[a-Elva Bhairavo
Raakssaseshvarah |
Indraakssii Devataa Tatra Indrennola-
Ulpaasitaa Puraa ||54||*

[At Lanka, my nupura, or anklet, fell. There the Bhairava is called Rakshaseshwara whose name literally means 'the lord of rakshasas'. The Devata (implying Devi) there is known as Indrakshi whose name literally means 'the eye of Indra'.]

The Shakti Peetha in Nainativu, Manipallavam, is a short distance from the ancient capital of Sri Lanka, Jaffna, in Nallur. The Devi here was worshipped by both Lord Rama and the powerful Lanka king, Ravana. Her idol was built by Indradev himself, who worshipped the divine Goddess here. It is believed that this is the spot where the Devi's anklet fell.

It is known to visiting pilgrims as Nainativu Nagapoosani Amman temple and is as ancient and historic as the town within which it exists. The Devi worshipped here is a form of Parvati, known locally as Nagapooshani or Bhuvaneshwari, and her consort, Lord Shiva, is worshipped as Rakshaseshwara or Nayanair. Since this was where the Devi's anklets fell, the significance of anklets in the worship of Shakti holds immense importance since time immemorial. The ornament has been revered and in the famous epic Tamilian poem about the Devi, 'Silapatikaram', the story begins and ends with this piece of jewellery.

As Bhuvaneshwari, she is the queen or the ruler of the universe, which is a role she fulfils as the divine mother. The entire universe thus can be viewed as her body and all beings, ornaments of that infinite being. Her flowering selfhood carries the world within her and as such, she is also related to Sundari or Rajarajeshwari, the supreme lady of the universe.

In Hinduism, Bhuvaneshwari Devi is one of the Dus Mahavidyas, and was the fourth celestial Goddess to appear. She is much like Kali or the Tri-Devi in her aspect, where she is the creator and destroyer of the universe, with everything beginning and ending within her. In certain sects of Shakta worship, Devi Parvati is seen as the sagun rupa of Devi Bhuvaneshwari and her bij mantra is 'Hreem'.

Locally it is believed that the Devi can grant any wish, as she wields the power of the Trimurti. As mentioned earlier, the Nainativu Nagapoosani Amman temple was originally consecrated by the Lord of the Heavens himself, Indradev, when he was seeking respite from the curse placed on him by Gautama Maharishi. In the epic poem Mahabharata, Lord Indra was overcome by desire for Gautama Maharishi's wife, Ahalya, and so he disguised himself as the sage and proceeded to seduce and make love to her. When the saint found out, he cursed Indra with having a thousand marks on his body resembling the yoni, or the female reproductive organ. Indra, ridiculed, was thus called sa-yoni; however, he went into exile to the island of Manidweepa (present-day Nainativu). Here he consecrated the temple to the Goddess and worshipped her moolasthana murti to atone for his sins. The Goddess, as the divine mother and

*Indrakshi Temple (Nagapooshani Amman Temple),
Nainativu, Sri Lanka
Photo: Creative Commons/Wikinamaste*

queen of the universe, satisfied by the Lord's repentance and penance, transformed the many yonis on his body into 1,000 eyes, from which she receives the name 'Indrakshi'.

The original temple was looted and destroyed by the Portuguese when they arrived on the island in 1620 CE, and the modern-day structure was built in 1788. The temple was attacked once again and severely damaged between 1958 and 1986 by the Sri Lankan forces, but has since been repaired.

The temple today is visited by pilgrims, devotees and travellers alike and it is believed that the Goddess smiles benevolently at all those who come to her shrine with a pure heart and devotion in their eyes.

50

Shivaharkaray Shakti Peetha
Karavipur, Karachi, Pakistan

Karaviire Tri-Netram Me Devii Mahissamardinii |
Krodhiisho Bhairavas-Tatra Sugandhaayaan-Ca
Naasikaa ||5||

[At Karavira, my trinetra or three eyes fell; where the Devi is Mahishamardini whose name literally means 'the destroyer of the demon Mahishasura', and the Bhairava there is Krodhisha whose name literally means 'one who is the possessor of anger'.]

The Shivaharkaray Shakti Peetha is located in the city of Karachi in Pakistan. Shivaharkaray, or Karavipur as it is known colloquially, is a Shakti Peetha that is dedicated to Goddess Durga, and is located at some distance from the Parkai railway station in Karachi. According to Puranic texts, this is where Devi Sati's three eyes fell and the Goddess worshipped here is Mahishasuramardini. Protecting her temple is her consort, Lord Shiva, in the form of his Bhairava, Krodhisha, who is the personification of anger. It is interesting to note that every form of Shiva's Bhairava has fearsome aspects related to war and anger, and is emblematic of the Lord's mental state at losing his consort, Sati. As the Peethas were consecrated by

Shiva, it was as though he left behind parts or aspects of himself with his Shakti, before embarking on a deep sadhana, to bring him out of which, Adi Shakti had to take on another human form to ensure that the world would be at an equilibrium again.

Shivaharkaray is the third Peetha in the list of 51 Shakti Peethas entailed in Adi Sankaracharya's seminal text about the Devi. There is a popular belief in the region that another temple dedicated to the Devi in the Indian city of Kolhapur in Maharashtra is where the Devi's trinetra, or three eyes, fell; however, Karavipur is widely accepted as the spot for this pind of the Devi. The closest Indian city to Karavipur is in Gujarat and the town is extremely well-connected, catering to pilgrims, devotees and travellers who go visiting there.

Mythologically, Durga was known as the slayer of Mahishasura, a demon who was born from a buffalo and was representative of man's primal animalistic instincts. When Mahishasura wreaked havoc in the world, the gods called upon the Devi to intervene and from their own persons, decked her in weapons of war, preparing her for the battle between good and evil. As Durga killed the demon who was a representation of base nature, she also brought an end to human qualities which keep us from attaining enlightenment, like ego, ignorance, greed and selfishness. She became Mahishasuramardini and was thus the Goddess who could dispel mortals from the trappings of the illusionary world. In this form, the Devi shows us the path to overcoming our primal nature and the lion that is her vahan is a representation of man's virility. The base nature has to be conquered and kept under control although never completely removed, since it is also this nature which allows for life to continue, for creation to exist. Every part has its role to play, but for spiritual enlightenment and the sake of divine creation, it is essential to tame it.

Alongwith Hinglaj, the Mahishasuramardini Shivaharkaray Peetha are two of the Shakti Peethas dedicated to the worship of the Goddess which are based in Pakistan. During Durga Puja, which is one of the most important festivals of the Goddess, the temple is decked up, and for the entire period of nine days, the Devi is worshipped with much aplomb. There is also the practice of a four-day procession, or teertha yatra, which is held in the month of April, for which people from all across the subcontinent gather in order to pay their respects to the Devi.

51

Chandrabhaga Shakti Peetha
Prabhas, Girna Hills, Gujarat

*Udaran-Ca Prabhaase Me Candrabhaagaa Yashasvinii |
Vakratunnddo Bhairava Uurdhvo[a-O]ssttho
Bhairavaparvate ||43||*

[At Prabhasa, my udara, or stomach, fell.
There the Devi is known as Chandrabhaga whose name literally means 'the portion of the moon'. She is beautiful and famous. The Bhairava is called Vakratunda whose name literally means 'with a curved body'.]

In Prabhas-khetra in Gujarat's Junagarh district, near the Somnath temple, it is believed that Devi Sati's stomach fell. Here the Goddess is worshipped as Chandrabhaga, or the moon goddess, alongside her Bhairava, Vakratunda, an aspect of the Lord Shiva, who is known as the one with the curved body. The Prabhas Shakti Peetha is located near the town of Veraval in Junagrah, a place where the Shakta tradition thrives in the community. The temple is a sacred place known for its spiritual significance as it is the place where the three holy rivers Hiran, Kapila and Saraswati connect and merge within the waters of one another.

The site of the temple is a short distance from the cosmopolitan city of Ahmedabad, the capital and prime commercial centre of the state of Gujarat and as such transportation and connectivity to the temple is excellent, making it easy for pilgrims, devotees and travellers alike to come visiting. A popular destination among the Shakta sect, each year the site sees a large number of visitors thronging to pay their respects to the Devi. With the Somnath temple dedicated to Lord Shiva being not too far away from the Devi's temple, one sees it as part of the Gujarat pilgrim circuit, with both temples being integral in the Uma-Shiva worship tradition.

There is a story in the Puranic texts where Chandra Deva, the Moon God, wanted to marry one of the daughters of King Daksha Prajapati, called Rohini, but along with her, married all 27 daughters of Daksha. Enraged, the king cursed the Moon to vanish from existence. Repenting for his error, the Moon prayed to Lord Shiva in order to bring back his light and the balance to the world. The Devi was the force who intervened and showed Chandra the path to earn back his presence in the world and it was as a result of this effort that the Somnath temple and the Devi's shrine as Chandrabhaga came to be. There is not a lot of information that one finds regarding the construction of the Somnath temple, but we know that it is an ancient construction because of the engravings and sculptures carved into the walls of the site.

Uniquely though, there is no actual shrine here dedicated to Devi Chandrabhaga. There is only a tradition of worship at the place where the three rivers meet, where Shakta worshippers meet for the darshan of the Devi. Here, absence in the form of an idol does not withhold her worship or her significance as the one laying the path to enlightenment, the seat of the Moon's power and thus the power of the divine feminine.

In the months of Navratras, during Ashwija masa, that is from September to October, and Chaitra masa, that is March to

April, there is a celebration of great vigour and devotion at the Prabhas Shakti Peetha. During these days, devotees worship the Goddess by not eating any food that is taken from the soil for the entirety of nine days. Another festival of great significance is Shivratri, and a magnificent fair is held at Somnath on the Kartik Poornima in the month of November every year. Men and women come together for the colourful dance performance of Garba or Dandiya during the nine nights of the Navratras.

Acknowledgements

This book is a divine gift. The belief in the divine has been ingrained in me ever since I can remember. It is the complete belief in the supreme energy that guides our lives—the Adi Shakti. This book is solely the idea of Dibakar Ghosh, Editorial Director of Rupa Publications. I am grateful for the trust and faith he reposed in me at every step of the way. He was always present whenever I wanted to embroider the concept and the writing. Debangana Banerjee's editing has given the book the nips and tucks it needed.

To my all-Shakti research team—Ipseta Sengupta, Dilpreet Bhullar and Girinandini Singh.

To my father Jagdish Chandra Pande, a devout Devi Chandi bhakta, who, through his various worship rituals, brought new insights into my understanding of the Great Goddess.

To Ravinder Rawat and Suprabha Nayak.

To my husband Mukul Joshi, and my sister Tripti P. Desai, who gave me the much-needed moral and emotional support during the writing of the book.

And, above all, my publisher Kapish Mehra, for all his energy and support.

Bibliography

Ali, Daud, (ed.) *Invoking the Past: The Uses of History in South Asia*, Oxford University Press, Delhi, 1999.

Anderson, Pamela Sue and Beverley, Clack, (eds.). *Feminist Philosophy of Religion: Critical Readings*, Routledge, London, 2004.

Appadurai, Arjun, Frank J. Korom and A. Margaret (eds.). *Gender, Genre and Power in South Asian Expressive Traditions*, Motilal Banarsidass, Delhi, 1994.

Basham, Arthur L., *Wonder That Was India* (Revised Edition.) London: Sidgwick & Jackson, 1967.

Avalon, Arthur. *Shakti and Shakta*, Mineola: Dover Publications Inc, 2016.

Bandopadhyay Rakhaldas. *Itihas: Pratham Khanda*, Nababharat Publishers, Calcutta, 1974.

Bandyopadhyay, Anil Chandra. *Madhyajuge Bangia O Bangali*, K. P. Bagchi & Co., Calcutta, 1986.

Bandyopadhyay, Kalyani. *Durgapuja Kalipuja: Itihaser Darpan*, Mitram, Kolkata, 2006.

Banerjea J.N. *The Development of Hindu Iconography*, Munshiram Manoharlal, New Delhi, 2002.

Banerji, S.C., *Tantra in Bengal: A Study in its Origin, Development and Influence*, Naya Prakash, Delhi, 1992.

Beane W.C., *Myth, Cult and Symbols in Sakta Hinduism: A Study of the Indian Mother Goddess*, EJ Brill, Leiden, 1977.

Benard, Elisabeth Anne. *Chinnamasta: The Aweful Buddhist and Hindu Tantric Goddess*, Motilal Banarsidass, Delhi, 1994.

Bera, G.K. *The Land of Fourteen Gods: Ethno-cultural Profile of Tripura*. Mittal Publications. p. 120. 2010.

Berkson, Carmel. *The Divine and the Demoniac: Mahisa's Heroic Struggle with Durga*, Oxford University Press, Delhi, 1995.

Bhattacharji, Sukumari. *Indian Theogony: A Comparative Study of Indian Mythology, from the Vedas to the Puranas*, Motilal Banarasidass, Delhi, 1988.

Bhattacharji, Sukumari. *Women and Society in Ancient India*, Basumati Corporation Limited, Calcutta, 1994.

Bhattacharya, Benoytosh. *The Indian Buddhist Iconography*, Firma KL Mukhopadhyay, Calcutta, 1958.

Boner, Alice, Sarma, Sadasiva Rath, and Silpa Prakasa. *Medieval Orissan Sanskrit Text on Temple Architecture.* Leiden: Brill. 1966.

Caldwell, Sarah. *Oh Terrifying Mother: Sexuality, Violence and Worship of Goddess Kali*, Oxford University Press, New Delhi, 2001.

Campbell, June. *Gender, Identity and Tibetan Buddhism*, Motilal Banarsidass, Delhi, 2003.

Chaitanya, Krishna. *Arts of India*, New Delhi: Abhinav Publications, 1987.

Chakrabarti, Kunal. *Religious Process: The Puranas and the Making of a Regional Tradition,* Oxford University Press, New Delhi, 2001.

Chatterjee, Rama. *Religion in Bengal: During the Pala and the Sena Times*, Punthi Pustak, Calcutta, 1985.

Chattopadhyaya, Brajadulal. *The Making of Early Medieval India*, Oxford University Press, New Delhi, 2006.

Chattopadhyaya, Debiprasad. *Lokayata: A Study in Ancient Indian Materialism*, People's Publishing House, Calcutta, 1959.

Chattopadhyaya, Sudhakar. *Evolution of Hindu Sects (Upto the Time of Sankaracharya)*, Munshiram Manoharlal, New Delhi, 1970.

Chitgopekar, Nilima (ed.). *Invoking Goddess: Gender Politics in Indian Religion*, Har-Anand Publication Pvt. Ltd., Delhi, 2002.

Chowdhury, Abdul Momin. *Dynastic History of Bengal (c. 750-1200 A.D.)*, The Asiatic Society of Pakistan, Dacca, 1967.

Chowdhury, P.C. *The History of the Civilization of the People of Assam to the Twelfth Century*, Gauhati,1966.

Christ, Carol P. *Rebirth of the Goddess: Finding Meaning in Feminist Spirituality*, Routledge, New York,1997.

Coburn, Thomas B. *Encountering the Goddess: A Translation of the*

Devi Mahatmya and a Study of Its Interpretation. Delhi: Sri Satguru Publications, 1992.

Coburn, Thomas, B., *Devi-Mahatmya: The Crystallization of the Goddess Tradition*. Motilal Banarsidass, Delhi, 1984.

Saraswati, S.N. *Sannyasa Darshan: A Treatise on Traditional and Contemporary Sannyasa*. Yoga Publications Trust, 2005.

Cooey, Paula M., William R. Eakin & Jay B. McDaniel (eds.). *After Patriarchy: Feminist Transformations of the World Religions*, Sri Satguru Publications, Delhi, 1996.

Coomaraswamy, A.K. *Essays in National Idealism*. Delhi: Munshiram Manoharlal, 1986.

Coomaraswamy, Ananda K. *Elements of Buddhist Iconography*. Third edition. New Delhi: Munshiram Manoharlal, 1979.

Coward, Harold. *Jung and Eastern Thought*, Sri Satguru Publications, New Delhi, 1991.

Das, H.C, *Iconography of Sakta divinities*, Vol. 2. Pratibha Prakashan, Delhi, 1997.

Dasgupta, Sashi Bhushan. *An Introduction to Tantric Buddhism*, University of Calcutta, Calcutta, 1974.

Dehejia, Vidya. *Devi: The Great Goddess: Female Divinity in South Asian Art*. Washington, DC: Sackler Gallery, 1999.

Doniger, Wendy. *Women, Androgynes, and Other Mythical Beasts*. Chicago and London: University of Chicago Press. 1980

Eck, D. L. (2012). *India: A Sacred Geography*. New York: Random House. p. 37. 2012.

Elgood, Heather. *Hinduism and the Religious Arts*, London: Cassell. 1999.

English, E. *Vajrayogini: Her Visualization, Rituals, and Forms*. Simon and Schuster. 2013.

Ghosh, Mallar. *Development of Buddhist Iconography in Eastern India: A study of Tara*, Munshiram Manoharlal, New Delhi, 1980.

Ghosh, Manomohan. Ed. and transl. *The Natya Sastra: A Treatise on Hindu Dramaturgy and Histrionics*. Calcutta: The Royal Asiatic Society of Bengal, 1950.

Gimbutas, Marija. *The Living Goddess*, University of California Press, Berkeley and Los Angeles, 1999.

Gopinath, Kaviraj. *"Nyaya-Vaisesika Philosophy,"* in *Aspects of Indian Thought*, 1979.

Goudriaan, Teun and Sanjukta Gupta. *Hindu Tantric and Sakta Literature*, Otto Harrsswitz, Wiesbaden, 1981.

Gupta, Chitralekha. *"Early Brahmanic Settlements in Bengal-Pre-Pala Period"*, in B.N. MukheIjee, D.R. Das, S.S. Biswas and S.P. Singh (eds), *Sri Dinesacandrika: Studies in Indology*, Sundeep Prakashan, Delhi, 1983.

Haase-Dubose, Danielle, John, Mary E., Marini, Marcelle, Melkote, Rama & Tharu, Susie (eds.) *French Feminism: An Indian Anthology*, Sage Publication, New Delhi, 2003.

Haque, Enamul. *Bengal Sculptures: Hindu Iconography upto C. 1250. A.D.*, Bangladesh National Museum, Dhaka, 1992.

Harper, Katherine Anne and Robert L. Brown. *Roots of Tantra*, State University of New York Press, Albany, 2002.

Hawley, John Stratton and Donna Marie Wulff (eds.), *Devi: Goddesses of India*, 1st Indian Edition 1998, New Delhi.

Hawley, John Stratton and Donna Marie Wulff (eds.) *The Divine Consort: Radha and the Goddesses of India*, Motilal Banarsidass, Delhi, 1982.

Hazra, R.C., *Studies in Puranic Records on Hindu Rites and Customs*, Motilal Banarsidas, Delhi,1975 (reprint).

Huntington Susan L., Huntington, John C. *The Art of Ancient India: Buddhist, Hindu, Jain.* New Delhi: Motilal Banarsidass. 2013.

Jacobsen, Knut A., *Prakrti in Yoga: Material Principle, Religious Experience, Ethical Implications*, Motilal Banarsidass, New Delhi, 2002.

Johnson, Allan G. *The Gender Knot: Unraveling Our Patriarchal Legacy*, Pearson Longman, New Delhi, 1997.

Joshi, M.C. "Historical and Iconographic Aspects of Sakta Tantrism" in *Explorations in Art and Archaeology of South India-Essays Dedicated to N.G. Majumdar*, ed., Y. Debala Mitra, Directorate of Archaeology and Museums and Government of West Bengal, Calcutta, 1996.

Jung, Carl Gustav, *Aspects of the Feminine*, Routledge, Indian edition, 2006

Rao, K.L. Seshagiri, Kapil Kapoor, Rajnish Kumar Mishra, Sadhvi

Bhagawati Saraswati, Santoṣa Kumara Shukla (ed.) *Encyclopedia of Hinduism* (11 Volume Set). New Delhi: Insight Collectibles. 2013.

Kakar, Sudhir and John M. Ross. *Tales of Love, Sex and Danger*, Oxford University Press, New Delhi, 1986.

Kakar, Sudhir. *The Analyst and the Mystic: Psychoanalytic Reflections on Religion and Mysticism*, Viking, New Delhi, 1991.

Kakati, Bani Kanta. *The Mother Goddess Kamakhya*, Lawyer's Book Stall, Guwahati, 1948, Third impression, 1967.

Keith, A.B. *The Sanskrit Drama in Its Origin, Development, Theory and Practice*. London: Oxford University Press, 1959.

Kemp, Sandra and Judith Squires (eds.) *Feminisms*, Oxford University Press, New York, 1997.

Kingsley, David. *Hindu Goddesses – Visions of the Divine Feminine in the Hindu Religious Tradition*, New Delhi: Motilal Banarsidass. 1998.

Kinsley, D. *Tantric visions of the Divine Feminine*. Delhi: Motilal Banarsidas. p. 207. 1998.

Kinsley, David R. "Kalf: Blood and Death Out of Place" in Hawley, John Stratton and Donham Marie Wulf (eds.), *Devi: Goddesses of India*, Motilal Banarsidass, Delhi, 1998

Kinsley, David R. *Hindu Goddess: Visions of the Divine Feminine in the Hindu Religious Traditions*, University of California Press, Berkley, 1975.

Kinsley, David R. *Tantric Visions of the Divine Feminine: The Ten Mahavidyas*, Motilal Banarsidass, Delhi, 1998.

Kinsley, David R. *The Sword and the Flute: Dark Visions of the Terrible and the Sublime in Hindu Mythology*, (Indian Reprint) Vikas Publishing House, Delhi, 1976.

McDaniel, June. *Offering Flowers, Feeding Skulls: Popular Goddess Worship in West Bengal: Popular Goddess Worship in West Bengal.* Oxford University Press, 2004.

McDermott, R. F., & Kripal, J. J. (Eds.). *Encountering Kali: In the margins, at the centre, in the west*. University of California Press. 2003.

McGee, Mary, (ed.) *Invented Identities: The Interplay of Gender, Religion and Politics In India*, Oxford University Press, Oxford, 2000.

Mishra, Nihar Ranjan. *Kamakhya: A Socio-Cultural Study*, D.K.

Printworld (P) Ltd., New Delhi, 2004.

Misra, Om Prakash. *Mother Goddess in Central India*, Agam Kala Prakashan, New Delhi, 1985.

Moi, Toril. *What is a Woman? and Other Essays*, Oxford University Press, Oxford, 1999.

Moitra, Shefali. *Feminist Thought: Androcentricism, Communication and Objectivity*, Munshiram Manoharlal in association with Centre for Advanced Studies in Philosophy, Jadavpur University, Kolkata, 2002.

Mookerjee, Ajit, Kalra. *The Feminine Force*, Thames and Hudson, London, 1988.

Ostor, Akos. *The Play of the Gods: Locality, Ideology, Structure and Time in the Festivals of a Bengali Town*, Chicago University Press, Chicago, 1980.

Padoux, Andre, "Tantrism: An Overview," in *Encyclopedia of Religion*, vol. 14, ed. by Mircea Eliade, Macmillan, New York, 1967.

Pal, Pratapaditya. "The Mother Goddesses according to Devipurana", Vol. XXX, No.1, January, 1988.

Pal, Pratapaditya, *Hindu Religion and Iconography*, Vichitra Press, Los Angeles, 1981.

Panikkar, S. *Saptamātrkā Worship and Sculptures: An Iconological Interpretation of Conflicts and Resolutions in the Storied Brāhmanical Icons* (No. 3). DK Printworld. 1997.

Pande, Alka. *Body Sutra: Tracing the Human Form Through Art & Imagination.* New Delhi: Rupa, 2019.

Pande, Alka. *Indian Art: The New International Sensation*, A Collector's Handbook, Bhopal: Manjul Publishing House Pvt Ltd, 2008.

Pande, Alka. *Masterpiece of Indian Art*, New Delhi: Lustre Press, Roli Books, 2004.

Pande, Alka. *Shringara: The Many Faces of Indian Beauty*, New Delhi: Rupa, 2010.

Pantel Pauline Schmitt. *A History of Women in the West: From Ancient Goddess to Christian Saints*, Bellknap Press of Harvard University Press, Cambridge, 1999.

Parasher, Aloka. *Mlechas in Early India: A Study in Attitudes Towards Outsiders Upto AD 600*, Munshiram Manoharlal, Delhi, 1991.

Pattanaik, Devdutt. *Devi: The Mother-Goddess: An Introduction.* Mumbai: Vakils, Feffer, and Simons Ltd. 2000.

Payne, Ernest A., "The Siktas: An Introductory and Comparative Study", Munshiram Manoharlal, New Delhi 1997.

Porselvi, P. Mary Vidya. *Nature, Culture and Gender: Re-reading the Folktale.* London: Routledge. 2016.

Preston, James J. (ed), *Mother Worship: Themes and Variations,* University of North Carolina Press, Chapel Hill, 1982.

Preston, James J. *Cult of Goddess; Social and Religious Change in Hindu Temple,* Vikas Publishing House, Delhi, 1980.

Przyluski, J., "The Great Goddess of India and Iran", Indian Historical Quarterly, No. 10. Sep. 3. 1934. Publishers Ltd., 1981.

Rajan, Rajeshwari Sundara. *Real and Imagined Women: Gender, Culture and Postcolonialism,* Routledge, New York, 1993.

Rao. T.A., *Elements of Hindu Iconography.* Delhi: Motilal Banarsidass, 1993.

Rawson, Philip. *The Art of Southeast Asia.* London: Thames and Hudson, 1967.

Renavikar, Madhavi D. *Religion and Women,* Rawat Publications, Jaipur, 2003.

Saraswati, S.K. *Tantrayana Art: An Album,* The Asiatic Society, Calcutta, 1977.

Saraswati, S. N. (2005). *Sannyasa Darshan: A Treatise on Traditional and Contemporary Sannyasa.* Yoga Publications Trust.

Sax, William S, (ed.) *The Gods at Play: Lila in South Asia,* Oxford University Press, New York, 1995.

Sengupta, Arputha Rani. *Cult of Goddess.* New Delhi: D.K. Printworld, 2015.

Shah, Kirit K. (ed.) *History and Gender: Some Explorations,* Rawat Publications, Jaipur, 2005.

Shah, Shalini. *The Making of Womanhood: Gender Relations in the Mahabharata,* Manohar, New Delhi, 1995.

Sharma, Arvind. (ed.) *Women in Indian Religions,* Oxford University Press, New Delhi, 2002.

Sinha, S.N. and N.K. Basu. *Women in Ancient India: Vedas to Vatsyana,* Khama Publishers, Delhi, 2002.

Sircar, Dinesh Chandra, (ed). *The Sakti Cult and Tara,* University of Calcutta, Calcutta, 1971.

Srinivasan, Doris. *Many Heads, Arms, and Eyes: Origin, Meaning, and Form of Multiplicity in Indian Art,* Leiden: Brill, 1997.

Starza, O.M. *The Jagannatha Temple at Puri: Its Architecture, Art, and Cult* (Vol. 15). Brill. 1993. p. 87.

Subramaniam, V. *Mother Goddesses and Other Goddesses,* Ajanta Publishers, Delhi, 1993.

Sunil V. *Ayurveda and Panchakarma: The Science of Healing and Rejuvenation.* Wisconsin: Lotus Press. p. 89. 1997.

Thadani, Giti. *Moebius Trip: Digressions from India's Highways,* Penguin Books, New Delhi, 2003.

Thapan, Meenakshi, ed. *Embodiment: Essays on Gender and Identity,* Oxford University Press, Delhi, 1997.

Thapar, Romila. *Sakuntala: Texts, Readings and Histories,* Kali for Women, New Delhi, 1999.

Thomas, P. *Kama Kalpa or the Hindu Ritual of Love.* Bombay: DB Taraporevala Sons and Co., 1959.

Tirumular, *Tirumantiram: A Tamil Scriptural Classic.* Chennai: Sri Ramakrishna Math. 1991.

Tiwari, J.N. *Goddess Cults in Ancient India* (with special reference to the first seven centuries AD), Sandeep Prakashan, Delhi, 1985.

Trivedi, R.D. *Iconography of Parvati, Agam Kala Prakashan,* Delhi, 1981.

Turner, Victor W. *The Ritual Process: Structure and Anti-structure,* Routledge and Kegan Paul, London, 1969.

Urquhart, Margaret M. *Women of Bengal,* Gyan Publishing House, Delhi, 1987.

Vaidyanathan, T.G. and Jeffrey J. Kripal, *Vishnu on Freud's Desk, A Reader in Psycho-analysis and Hinduism,* Oxford University Press, New Delhi, 1999.

Vaudeville, Charlotte. *Myths, Saints and Legends in Medieval India,* Oxford University Press, New Delhi, 1996.

Venkataraman, K.R. *Devi Kamakshi in Kanchi: A Short Historical Study,* R. A. Sattanathan, The Modern Stores, Tirucherapally, 1973.

Waddel, L.A. *The Tribes of Brahmaputra Valley: A Contribution on their*

Physical Types and Affinities, Sanskaran Prakashak, Delhi, 1975.

Wadley, Susan Snow. *Shakti: Power in the Conceptual Structure of Karimpur Religion*, Munshiram Manoharlal, Delhi, 1985.

Warrier, S. *Kamandalu: The Seven Sacred Rivers of Hinduism*. Mayur University. p. 34. 2014.

Sri Lalita Sahasranama Stotram available online at https://www.manblunder.com/articlesview/sri-lalita-sahasranama-stotram, accessed on June 20, 2020.

Guhyak Strotam, available online at, https://sanskritdocuments.org/doc_Devii/guhyakAlIsahasranAmastotram.html?lang=iast accessed on May 27, 2020

Saraswati Mantra available at http://sanskritslokas.com/saraswati-mantra/page-1.html, accessed on May 29, 2020.

Tara Strotam available at https://greenmesg.org/stotras/tara/tara_stotram.php, accessed on July 20, 2020.

Shakti Peeth available at https://greenmesg.org/stotras/durga/shakti_peethas.php, accessed on August 3, 2020.

Maheswara strotam available at https://stotranidhi.com/en/uma-maheshwara-stotram-in-english/, accessed on September 3, 2020.

Devi Mahatomyaya available at https://sanskritdocuments.org/doc_Devii/devImAhAtmyastotram.html?lang=sa, accessed on Septmber 2, 2020.